Blurbs

"Touches that tight sweet spot between right now and the next technical leap with so little effort, one is left with the uncomfortable feeling he may be writing this from the future."

John Kipling Lewis
Author
"Unselected"

"Intriguing writer! He can use strong short sentences that bind you to his story immediately. How does he do that?"

Juliëtte van Bavel
Artist and Sculptor
www.kunstenares.eu

Copy Me

Copy Me

by

LASTON KIRKLAND

Published by (S+)
S+ Press
P.O. Box 5741
Oak Ridge, TN 37831

www.splus.press

Library of Congress Cataloging-in-Publication Data
Kirkland, Laston
[Short stories]
Copy me: & other science fiction stories / Laston Kirkland.–1st ed.
p. cm.
ISBN-13 978-0692303719
ISBN-10 0692303715
1. Kirkland, Laston, 1965–. 2. Science Fiction, American. I. Title

Library of Congress Control Number: 2014919262
S+ Press, Oak Ridge, Tennessee

Cover design and photograph by Meg Tufano

Manufactured in the United States of America

First Edition

This book is dedicated to my wife, Jenn, and three daughters, Leanna, Abby, and Lizzy, who are singing to each other in the background as I write this, and warming my heart.

CONTENTS

Human

Ronald hated his job, sometimes.

Sure it was a necessary thing but even so. He hated this part.

She was not wearing her diagnostics patch. She had refused to come in for evaluation, and the sensors in her car were reporting it rarely moved. He did check with the house cloud, using his override code, and it reported that SOMEONE was definitely moving around in there. Water and power fluctuated on the meters.

She had set her communications to private. She wore old AR glasses. Those old glasses didn't have any responder signals. All he could tell was they moved around the house and grounds.

A whole house and a garden. Wealthy. Part of his job would be to catalog and assess the value and arrange to distribute the assets.

He sometimes wished the medical privacy act of '36 had never occurred, or he would have been able to just check her records to see what work had been done, then run an inference program. But no medical device except a patch was allowed to transmit and no medical information could be stored. It did cut down on prejudice, but now you needed the patch. Especially on old people. He could run illegal applications as a lot of people did but he was official. Not allowed. As an official, everything he saw while on duty was automatically filed. His vision registered in public records attached to his serial number.

Officially, you had to patch people. It was the law.

Since she wouldn't talk to anyone online, someone had to go and check up on her and see if she counted. Her son and grandson were lost years ago and she had no other family. It was up to him to determine what was next for her.

The sidewalk came right up to the front of the house. It was free of dirt or decay, but that just meant it had probably been coated with a hydrophobe. Nothing really got dirty anymore. Or rusty. Or weathered.

On the step, he checked his map, two on tall building perches, and five in hover patterns. There were seven police drones within call range if he needed help. She could be a rogue or something. If she was, he'd need all the help he could get.

He rang the doorbell, waited, knocked loudly, waited, and knocked again. No response. He sighed. This might be a bad one. "Mrs. Wilson! I know you are home." He wasn't really expecting an answer. He scanned the area with his new eyes, infrared and ultraviolet. He frowned as his UV app glitched out a bit. Pixelation. Unheard of. He might need an adjustment to his eyes. He hoped that it wouldn't take long. He'd pop in later to a hospishop and get it done.

"Go away!"

The voice startled Ronald, it was strong and firm and much closer than he had expected. Still, a good sign. She certainly sounded like she was healthy and aware.

"Mrs. Wilson. I'm Ronald Danner. I'm your caseworker." He felt a little awkward talking through the door.

"Jacob Wassisname is my caseworker."

"No, Jacob Weisse quit over a year ago. I picked up his case-load, and have sent you multiple messages which you ignored, and two physical certified letters, which you refused to sign for." He made a mental note that the name of her caseworker was forgotten. Another good sign, actually, unless this was deliberate fraud.

"Fine fine. So you're my caseworker. Go away!"

"Mrs. Wilson, I have to run an evaluation, I need you to wear a patch and I have to vouch for you."

"I'm fine. Lost the patch somewhere, slip the damn thing in the mail slot, and I'll put it on."

"No, Mrs. Wilson, I have to run a series of tests, I have to. If you don't cooperate, I'll be forced to call for police.Now, unlock your door, and we will do the evaluation that way, OK? You are a hundred and twenty six years old. We have to do an evaluation every year now. Your house is covered by the Honored Elders Act, as are the grounds and all your posses-sions. But part of the deal is we have to do the evaluation."

"I'm talking to you. Why do you need more proof than that?"

Ronald looked up at the sky, "Because my voicemail can have

THIS conversation, Mrs. Wilson. We've had vocal response software for decades. "He sighed again. This is why he hated this part. "It's the law Mrs. Wilson. I have to. I have to prove you are still human." Ronald paused, "And still alive."

For the longest time, there was silence. Just as Ronald was reaching up to gesture for a drone and run a lock override, the door opened.

Mrs. Wilson was standing there, neatly dressed and clean which Ronald thought was another good sign. She still cared what she looked like.

She had that slightly grey-blue skin tone of those who had been rejuvenated. Very smooth. No wrinkles. Her AR glasses were old, the kind that had a set of digital eyes projected onto the front, a common trick twenty years ago. Most AR gear were implants nowadays. It was a one percent operation and everyone did it. His own eyes were top-of-the-line.

He could already tell she would pass the tests. She didn't look more than ten percent–tops.

"Do I look dead to you?"

"No ma'am, but a visual inspection doesn't fly, not since the the Shade Tree Retirement Village scam of '43."

Ronald had helped document that one. Sixty branch offices, four hundred retirement communities, ten thousand walking dead–so many of them were over 90 percent–dead ten years or more. He would have shuddered if he could. Some of the lawsuits were still being processed to this day. The case was integral to the Fifty Percent Inheritance and Social Security Reform Act.

"Imagine that. You with your shiny skin and big bug eyes! Making me have to prove I'm human. Fine, do your tests."

"Out here?"

She stepped back and gestured to the dining room.

As he walked inside Ronald was appalled at how much STUFF old people had. Shelves full of physical things that served no purpose other than decoration or to trigger memories. There were TWO blankets on the couch and images behind physical glass were stuck to all the walls. She kept FOUR chairs around the table, even though Ronald knew he was likely the first person in the home in years. It made a lot more sense just to print the chairs when you needed them, as many as you need and recycle them later. She probably had a dozen cups and plates and glasses and eating utensils. Old people always did that. He didn't understand why.

She sat quietly as he administered the tests even though she was glaring at him. The patch on her clavicle was applied easily enough. He checked the readings. It measured heart rate, oxygen levels, DNA, the chemicals present in her sweat and skin. Her electrical impulses mapped to exquisite detail. She had magnetic resonance, sonogram, and passive x-ray.

Her lungs had at one point been replaced but were full biological, grown from her own cells. That must have cost a fortune. One of her kidneys was mechanical. A functioning organ that worked well, replacing it with bio made little sense, and cost so much. Her skin had been replaced, that was obvious. It caused the grey color, but removed all the wrinkles, blemishes, and any sagging. A little nano in the blood, probably just respirocytes and hyper whites, very common. Only a few failing organs that would need replacing in a year or two and she might want to add a little nano to her bones, some osteoporosis that needed reversing. OK. Things were looking OK.

Looks like she was only eight percent cyborg. That was well within accepted range. Ronald wouldn't need to do anything. Great news. Ronald himself was thirty percent. He'd replaced his skin years ago for a composite of silicon and tungsten with a digital layer allowing high resolution pigmentation and projection. Looked great, better than bio. And he didn't have a heart beat having replaced his heart with a continuous flow pump. With that and a good pair of augmentation eyes, a memory implant and a meshlink? He had the same quality make and model respirocytes Mrs. Wilson did and so he knew they both were good to go for a long, long time.

He was careful, not anywhere near fifty percent. He was smart not to swap out too much of his brain. Everyone knew the legal limits. Get near those numbers? You might lose the ability to call yourself human anymore. Not Ronald, no way! Inheritance rules took immediate effect, estate sales were done, taxes collected. Of course only the VERY wealthy could afford bio. But if you were careful, good replacements almost never wore out.

And what was the worst that could happen anyway? Most cyborgs considered it a fair trade. Immortality vs. the loss of material possessions? He'd deal with that when he got there. But it was strange how some people thought it was so important. OK, this was a good day. No need for any changes. Ronald was satisfied. She'd be keeping her stuff. He checked her patch. It was working fine. Time to get on with the next job.

He was glad things had worked out. He hated having to tell some people they didn't count as human anymore. Some just didn't take it very well.

Or worse, there were those who had extensive modifications, including memory and speech implants. It was hard trying to convince a cyborg that they had died! They tended to just go through the motions, following subroutines that had once been habits. Dead, but moving around. Zombies, really.

On those days, Ronald would have to find out if any personality or autonomous thought still existed in the cyborg corpse. If not, then he might have to call for some back-up. Rare. Then it was pretty easy. Just upload a control program and walk with the body to an assessment center, where they would determine if the cyborg parts could or should be recycled. He could file the paperwork in his sleep he'd done it so many times and just go about recovering and redistributing any assets they had. In the old days, it was even easier, they used to bury them intact. But other people were digging them up for spare parts. That's when the Graverobber Act of '40 made it illegal to bury recoverable augmentation. Just made common sense. Why waste a perfectly good silicon and tungsten? That stuff was NOT cheap!

His toughest days were if he found autonomous thought in someone over fifty percent, then the cyborg would be declared sentient but no longer human. Ronald tried not to think about those days. It would be sent to join an enclave of other AI's, its personality merged with many others to keep it from going rogue and becoming an anomaly danger. Lucky for him, that was not his job. Ronald turned when the patch program, "dinged."

Job was done, time to go. No danger of Cyborg or death with Mrs. Wilson. As he logged out of the diagnostics, he looked around the amazing clutter of the house and idly asked her, "Why don't you go outside anymore Mrs. Wilson?"

"Oh, I hate it out there, everyone a cyborg, silver and gold, weird looking. Clothes painted on and everyone everywhere connected and talking to each other but never out loud. Nope, I'm staying in my house."

"So what do you do all day?"

She glared at him defiantly, "I play with my grandson, Jim."

Ronald went quiet, his display was showing him that Jim Wilson had died at the age of sixteen. "Excuse me?"

"I spend at least two hours each day playing with Jim. Usually longer. I raised him when his father died."

Ronald checked the patch, no tell tale signs of dementia, schizophrenia, or hallucinogens. She had no brain implants and the EEG readings indicated normal patterns.

He looked up at her, intrigued. "Explain."

"Your fancy eyes do old-school wimax four transfers?"

Ronald checked. "Yes, it's supported."

"My son David was very into AR back when it was new. We were the first people to get these glasses and we put cameras up in every room. David and his wife died when Jim was still a baby. This is May 16th, 2019, when Jim took his first steps."

Ronald accepted the signal and gasped. Suddenly the entire house looked brand new. Crawling on the floor, surrounded by cloth and plastic toys, was a baby. Looking and sounding real.

He was quite used to video feeds, but for the last thirty years or so, such signals were deliberately translucent and off color, to aid in differentiating reality from imagery. These old glasses were displaying a level of quality that had been illegal for years. Ever since the AR virus attacks of the '40's, it was absolutely forbidden to make any sensory recording indistinguishable from reality. By the end of that decade only illegal equipment even had the capability. This legacy stuff was the most valuable tech he'd ever seen before. But it wasn't illegal, not if you bought it when it came out. Still.

The baby stood up from the toys, cooed, looked directly at Ronald and wobbled very slowly toward him. Just before he toppled over onto the wooden floor, Ronald reached out to catch him. The baby fell right through his hands. It had been a long time since he'd even seen a baby. They were so rare. The licensing requirements alone were so expensive.

Mrs. Wilson picked the crying child up or at least pretended to, holding her hands as if she was carrying the squalling child and began to croon to him. He quieted down and then the baby laughed. Now there was a sound you don't hear every day, Ronald thought. She stopped suddenly and looked directly at Ronald. With a gesture the room was back to its slightly dilapidated and aged state.

Ronald blinked again. He wasn't used to this level of detail.

"Wow!" Ronald looked at her. He was going to tell her how much all this legacy stuff was worth but before he could speak, she interrupted him–

"Let me show you July 3rd, 2021, fireworks."

A small boy, blonde with curly hair, was jumping up and down and looking up at Ronald with wide eyes, "Fowwoks! Gramma! I hear pop pop pop." And so did Ronald, a staccato sizzling sound from outside.

Mrs. Wilson smiled and said in exact lip sync to the projected image, "Yes Jim, but the real fireworks happen tomorrow." A loud explosion happened nearby making Ronald jump. Jim squealed and clapped his hands, running to the window, "Fowwoks!"

Ronald walked over to the window, marvelling at how seamless the video was, matching his every movement.Jim was perfect, even as he moved to angle his vision in unusual ways, looking for some evidence of rendering. When he looked out the window, he could see the same fireworks going off in the distance. A dozen people firing explosives into the air in an empty lot across the street. That had been outlawed forever. He'd never seen such a thing.

Again the child vanished. Across the street where the lot used to be was an apartment hostel, two hundred identical twenty by twenty by ten rooms. Arranged in three floors. Ronald lived in one very much like them.

Mrs. Wilson looked at Ronald, "There were sixty-five cameras in the house and another twenty-six in the back yard. I've recorded and stored every moment I had with Jim." Mrs. Wilson took her glasses off for a moment, showing ancient and sunken eyes. Skin transplants never seemed to really work around the eyes. The patch had pointed out that they worked fine but, aesthetically, Ronald thought she might want to get them replaced. "Let's go into the garden."

As they walked into the backyard, Ronald could see ancient fruit trees surrounded by patches of dozens of different herbs and perennial vegetables, walking paths of brick and ground-cover. This was an old garden, full of lots of hybrids and heritages. Ronald spotted at least ten hexapod robots tending the plants, none of them larger than a cat. It smelled wonderful. "You know, you might want to get a DNA catalog done of this place, you could have an unregistered gene sequence, if they find one, you could be wealthy."

Mrs. Wilson just gave him an annoyed look. "I did that twenty years ago. I had thirty seven new catalog entries, one viable enough that it was sold to one of the colonies. They grow my cucumbers on the moon."

She made the same gesture as before and Ronald accepted another input. Mrs. Wilson said, "This was September 25th, 2027."

Again the sudden shift in reality. A young boy hung upside down on a much younger apple tree, "Gramma I'll get you a good one!"

"You be careful now," came a sound that seemed to come

out of Ronald, but echoed by Mrs. Wilson, standing by him.

Jim monkeyed up the tree in total fearlessness, grabbing apples and tossing them down. Ronald watched as slender arms coming out of his own chest caught them and put them in a basket. He took a step to the left, and Jim adjusted his aim, throwing the apples to him. Ronald started to shuffle and dodge. Jim giggled, and threw harder, again the slender arms of a younger Mrs. Wilson caught each and every one.

Jim slipped and fell, bouncing off branches on the way down, thumping down in a crashing, flailing chaos of arms and legs. Ronald moved toward Jim in unison with the image super imposed upon him.

Jim recovered on the last branch and landed with his legs under him. He tucked into a roll and popped up with a "Tada!"

Ronald felt something like relief. Mrs. Wilson's scolding words came out of his mouth.

She led him from one room to another, in and out of the backyard, showing bits and snatches of her life with Jim. Helping him with schoolwork, his first date, playing board games, arguing over chores, whispering secrets.

She explained that she had enough footage of Jim, in so much detail, that the computers embedded in her home could even easily render situations and scenarios that never actually happened. So, she could pick a day, any day, and have any number of encounters with Jim, mixed and looped and rendered.

Finally, she showed him an image of a confident young teen, smiling as he waved behind him, "Don't wait up, Gramma, gonna be awhile before I come home." With that, Jim left the house with a spring in his step.

"Jim died in a violent attack, twenty minutes later. An explosive. It wasn't targeted at him. The bomber was protesting against the loss of jobs to robots."

"No footage of Jim exists after that, of course." Ronald knew from the file that the damage rendered Jim over sixty percent cyborg, including a good chunk of his brain. Almost no memory or perception, but the rest was good enough to continue functions so he'd been sent out to merge. Ronald could not remember where.

"He's part of a gestalt in New Mexico now, sharing consciousness with some six hundred other cyborgs. He may be still walking, but Jim died that day. I even went to see him once. He didn't recognize me, of course. As part of a collective he doesn't really think, he's just a mobile platform really. He's over 90 percent now. They just kept the brain stem."

She continued, "Any rendering I try doesn't feel right past that point. So I can have Jim at any moment in his life up until that moment."

"As you can see, Ronald Danner, I'm perfectly fine. My health is good. I don't leave the house much anymore because Jim can't come with me. I have not modified my mind or my body too much and I still count as human."

Ronald nodded as he left, "You most certainly do, Mrs. Wilson. You most certainly do. Thank you, it was really quite pleasant playing with Jim. I enjoyed this very much. Life was so very different back then. Have a good day."

Ronald loved his job, sometimes.

He wondered if he could request the time be removed from public records, he could maybe sell his afternoon with Jim and Mrs. Wilson. It sure was a rare experience to have had such high quality AR that wasn't illegal as hell. He'd call it, "Playing with Jim." Maybe it wasn't legal, he'd have to check it out.

As soon as Mrs. Wilson closed the door, her image shimmered and faded. A desiccated husk stood there. Tubes pumping nutrients into various mechanical components, very little flesh remained. A full ninety percent cyborg. The brain long ago devoid of thought. Used only for processing now.

Jim, now the house computer, did the AI equivalent of a sigh. Cameras watched Ronald walk away. He'd been preparing for this visit since Ronald first overrode his first level of security to scan for movement.

It was getting harder to hack the video streams of visitors. Lucky for Jim, Ronald Danner had full video and auditory implants. Jim had tracked his public feed down and replicated it. Then managed to intercept the feed of Ron's eyes just in time. The real problem is faking the UV spectrum, but other than that, he'd had no trouble.

After that it didn't matter anymore what Ronald saw. Jim got to the patch just in time to synthesize correct results for all of the data on his grandmother. He had to keep Ronald unaware and physically present while he processed it all. He had to build a fully virtual patch that would happily upload signal for years to come of Mrs. Wilson, in perfect health. Then get Ronald to accept the new inputs.

If he had not done that, then social inspector/insurance claims adjuster Danner would have taken her away and dismantled her. And then he would have dismantled the house, redistributing the assets. Then he would have merged Jim's AI personality with others to prevent anomalies.

He needed the house. It was important. If they took it away, how could he play with his grandmother?

☞

A Little Pot

Matt sat on one side of the table in his boxers and socks looking contrite. His pants were neatly folded on a bench behind him, next to his shirt. On the other side of the table were three members of airport security looking aggressive. On the table were three plastic baggies and four film canisters, each canister a different color.

"It's not what you think," said Matt.

"I think you had those hidden in your pants," said Guard One.

Guard Two added, "Yeah." Guard Three nodded.

"Okay, well it is what you think, but they aren't drugs. Uh, I mean, not all, I mean–"

"–Well, let's just see what they are then, shall we?"

Guard One reached out for the nearest of the baggies. Two said, "Yeah." And Three, he nodded.

Hmmm. Matt was noticing a bit of a pattern.

One opened the baggie. "Seeds?"

Matt looked over to Two, who obliged him with, "Yeah, looks like seeds."

Three nodded, again.

"Listen, these are apple seeds from an engineered strain I've been working on. See, once we fully mapped the genome, we got a far more viable strain. I've been talking for months with a bunch of people from all over the world and I need to get them samples. But it's illegal to mail home-grown fruit or even seeds without filling out forms. The fees are impossible–"

"–Uh, so why were you sneaking them on a plane?" interrupted One.

"Yeah, why?"

Nod.

"Well, honestly, I didn't think I'd get caught but also the smuggling fines for controlled substances are a lot less than the filing fees for my bio-hacked seeds. Do you know how much paperwork and money would be involved if I tried to mail these? It's much cheaper for me to book a flight and bring them myself."

"What's bio-hacked? The seeds?" One asked. "Did you make them into, like, cocaine apples or something?"

"Yeah, cocaine apples?"

Nod.

"No!" Matt shook his head. "What I did was more difficult. These particular seeds produce five times as many apples per tree than average. That allows the tree to pollinate itself twice a year and the apples, man they taste delicious! Oh, and the wood trunk grows twice as fast and three times as thick around as a normal apple tree so it makes great furniture, too! And, the thing that makes it even greater, it will grow in sandy salty soil!" Matt smiled.

Then he added with an attempt to sound humble, "I've signed my name in the DNA of the seeds."

"That doesn't sound bad. So that's all that these baggies and canisters contain? Apple seeds?"

"Yeah, just apple seeds?" Two was starting to get on Matt's nerves.

Matt realized Three had not nodded. *Hmmmm.* Three was looking at the seeds, then he spotted Matt watching him. He looked a little embarrassed and, again, as if it was a required part of his job, he nodded.

"No, actually, they're not all apple seeds. The blue canister holds a couple of peach pits modified the same way. The white canister has cherries and the black one has walnuts. I used the same variant on all of them. The red canister came from a friend who wants them for his lab. It's got spores bio-hacked to produce high protein mushrooms. While the—"

"—Aha! Shrooms!"

"Yeah, shrooms!"

Nod.

Matt sighed.

"No, not hallucinogens, these mushrooms taste a lot like pork. They grow the same way as mushrooms do everywhere, wet soil, in the dark." Matt grew more excited as he explained, "A bushel of these has the same nutritional value as a pig and makes a MUCH smaller environmental footprint. You can grow a crop every couple 'a weeks! Mix them with some non-modified amaranth paste—uh, that baggie over there has those seeds—and you even get the same texture as pork or chicken! They make great breaded nuggets!"

One, Two and Three stared at Matt.

"OK. So, what's in that last baggie?"

"Yeah, that last one."

Nod.

"Oh, just a little marijuana."

At that the room got quiet. Matt still was on the one side of the table, the three airport security guards on the other. All of them staring at the pot. Finally, One said, "Watch him. I'm gonna make a call and find out what to do about this.""Yeah, boss"

Nod.

Matt sat still in his underwear waiting for One to come back. No movement. No talking.

One returned and began stuffing the baggies and canisters into a paper sack. "Here's the deal. You may get dressed and leave. We will confiscate and destroy the bio-hazardous materials."

"All of it?" asked Matt.

"No sir," said One. "You may keep the marijuana. Enjoy your trip."

☞

His One Chance

The instructions read, "Determine where the Secondary Controls are on your model of vehicle. They should be beneath the Speed Indicator on the Dashboard."

Speed Indicator. *Hmmm.*

John Donny looked over the instructions again. It had been hard for him to get these instructions. He glanced up at his car controls, something he could hardly remember doing before.

Ah. He found the "Speed Indicator." That wasn't so hard!

Hmmm. It's showing mph and kph. Gee, he thought idly, We still measure miles on these things?

He got back to it. He looked at the dashboard again, frowning. He could see there was the air conditioning stuff, the music settings, privacy, viewscreen projector, the chair heat and massage, the netpad.

Wow. Lots of things on here!

He'd been so used to using his voice command, he'd forgotten you could do this all by touch. He'd need touch for this, though. The instructions made it clear you couldn't do it the easy way.

"Secondary Controls. Where are Secondary Controls?" he muttered under his breath. It must have been years since he'd looked at the panel. His car heard him muttering, and—to be helpful—enlarged and circled the button he sought on the dashboard screen. John's eyes widened, and he clamped his teeth together tight. I've got to be more careful, he thought to himself. I can't even sub-vocalize. He knew this was it, his one chance.

He scratched his head then looked up and out the window. Traffic was going as fast as always. An unbroken grid of cars packed so tightly together you could stand on one and step to another. Well, you could if—

His thoughts were interrupted by what he was seeing inside

a car on his right, a couple passionately embracing. After a few seconds, the girl saw him watching, gave him a look of annoyance, and toggled the privacy setting. All her windows turned instantly opaque. John gave a guilty start, then chuckled to himself. *I don't give a damn about your fun time, woman.* The slight ironic grin fell from his face as he was brought back to what he was doing. *You know what? You're probably the one.*

John looked down at the printed instructions again. When he was peaking, he was smarter than his friend Paul, but still, he didn't have the skill with all the systems his buddy had access to. It would have been irritating as hell except Paul showed him how he did it. John now had all the access he needed. Paul tweaked systems all the time, and let people use his profile. Considering sharing one's profile was so dangerous, John wasn't sure why Paul did it. But maybe it was because Paul had never been caught. He just didn't understand the chances he was taking.

Most important, Paul explained the override code for a car. He showed John how to change the default settings so Paul's access would override the car's automation. For Paul, it was just a, "Hey check this out!" For John, this was the key he had been looking for.

He felt a little bad about betraying Paul, but everyone knew people shouldn't be doing this sort of thing. It kinda served him right for being so careless with something as important as your profile.

With Paul's proxy, he could not only access Paul's work systems, he also had done the search that had sent a physical copy of the instructions to Paul's desk. He had taken the copy from Paul's Maker. Paul said he didn't mind at all. So using Paul, he changed the defaults.

John knew his own profile would have reported him. His psychological indicators, the recent breakup with his girl-friend, not to mention the promotion rejection from last week. If he had printed this from his own desk, or even used his own profile on Paul's, it would have raised a flag.

Last week, they'd upped his mandatory meds on the pill pump, he could feel it right away. Changing him.

Thing was, if they noticed it wasn't working, they would send someone to check up on him. Well, he wasn't going to let them find him!

Of course everybody had a profile. It started out as a way to keep track of friends, back when the Net was young. But then it grew. Every data-base's information merged and formed a guide that told everybody else who you were. Couldn't get a job without it matching your profile. Couldn't get a date, or buy a house, or a car. Your profile was your password, your access, your portal to everything. Everything came from it, and everything went through it.

His profile had words floating around it like, "Poor Impulse Control," "Manic-Depressive," "Attention Deficiency," "Low Empathy," and "Creative Type." Each one then fixed to the standard regulation levels by the pump.

He just could not go back on the pump! He hated that more than anything. Sure it got rid of his lows. But it got rid of his highs too. That damned pump, the size of a thumbnail, just under his armpit. Regulated his hormones. It used his own blood to make the levels match the standards, modified his blood stream directly. It took instructions from his profile.

People told him it was a marvel, but he didn't want his damned hormones regulated! He needed to be able to dance all night, to rule the world, to make every moment magic. God he loved the manic side. On that fucking pump everything mellowed out and stabilized. He could work, but he couldn't FEEL. Sure, he could do without the lows; but he just had to have those highs. He was willing to pay the price. He didn't want to be "fixed."

He looked up and out at the other cars again.

The one on his right still had the privacy settings on. He could imagine what they were doing now. The car in front had privacy too. The people inside were probably taking a nap. No, wait, the car might be empty, returning home after dropping off a passenger. No, he thought, An empty car would not do.

The one on his back bumper had five kids in it. The kids had folded the seats into the floor, and were in a circle playing some board game. Their mother had probably bundled them into the car and told it to go to grandmother's house. None of the kids looked old enough for their command voices to work on a car's nav system. Not the kids.

He had disabled his pill pump just two days ago. He had felt for the little lump, then used a pair of needle-nose pliers to squeeze the hell out of it. He'd had to print the pliers out, hadn't had a pair in so long. Model 45661 from a company named Sears. He was rather pleased with how well they worked, he had looked on the Net to find what the best tool was for squeezing, and the form factor looked perfect. He felt so in control when he used them!

He still had the bruises. A big purple splotch where he'd squeezed the pointy output end shut. He was actually pretty proud of the bruises. Breaking a pill pump without letting his profile know he'd done it was pretty amazing.

He felt a little sorry about what he was planning on doing. No one had done this in so long, it would flash all over the Net. His name would be legendary. He didn't want it to be the kids. So, that left the couple.

"From the Secondary Control screen, access the Physical Dropdown."

Wow! he thought, *Dropdowns, how quaint!* He silently thanked the bureaucracy for still requiring human controls. There. There's the menu: "Physical."

He had been on the best high he had ever had. It was epic. He walked the world like a god. Every man envied him; every woman wanted him. He could do anything. It was all so easy. He knew he didn't have much time left before the high vanished, and the low set in. He'd be crying and rocking in a heap for a couple days, and then refuse to leave his bed for a week. His profile would notice sooner rather than later, and then he'd be back on the pump. Now or never. Pay the price.

"Select Vehicular Controls."

He held his breath when he punched the button, expecting it all to happen right then. The car stayed rock steady, but with a click and a whirr something popped out of his dashboard very much like the gamepad he used on his entertainment wall at home. He exhaled slowly. Okay, so that's how to do it. He looked at it. Pretty easy, he thought. Push forward to go faster; pull backward to slow down or reverse; tilt to turn. Nothing to it. The buttons were probably important; but he didn't think he'd need them.

He knew that people used these all the time back in the day. They'd evolved from mechanical linkages that were, by some clever engineering, directly attached to the engine and wheels. He remembered all of that had made the cars fantastically expensive, too. Not like today where everyone had a service agreement, and a branded car would appear when you needed it.

Holding the car's manual controls he realized his seat wasn't right. He used his voice command: "Seat up. More. More. Stop. Seat tilt. Back. Back. Stop!" He put the seat right in the middle, so he could see out of every window. It seemed like the right way to do it. There. He was ready. He glanced at the paper again.

"From same menu, access Manual Override."

Manual Override. This was it. He'd only have a few seconds before a police monitor found a higher security profile. But John had fairly high clearance from his job. This was it. His moment of glory.

He touched the menu.

The car lurched and shuddered. John needed to steady the control pad. It didn't take long to get in full control, It was easier than he thought. The controls were a dream. At that same moment, all the cars around him swerved away, quite a distance away. He was now the only vehicle in the center of a large empty bubble, all other vehicles at least five meters distant. The traffic was still bumper to bumper inches away from each other, but his car was alone.

He hadn't expected that. He swerved as hard as he could to the right, his car's gyroscopic commands preventing him from flipping the car, but his reactions were no match against the other vehicles' automatic controls. They all swerved in unison, staying on all sides of him exactly the same five meter distance. He came nowhere near to hitting them.

The privacy window went off from the couple, holding their clothing in modesty. They were watching his car in astonishment. He tried again, the couple realized what he was doing, and fear filled their faces. But then they grinned when they saw that John couldn't get any closer to them. The girl gave him the finger.

In a wordless cry of frustration John twisted the control as hard as he could the other direction. His gyroscopic systems easily kept all four wheels on the ground but wrenched him hard against the inside of his door. But he couldn't hit anything! The car with the kids in it was still behind him. All five had their faces pressed against the glass. Fine. Them.

John pulled as much as he could on his control pad, and his car stopped as hard as it would let him. Automatic systems took over the manual and slowed him safely down to a complete stop in fractional seconds. They worked so well, there weren't even any marks on the road.

The vehicle with the kids easily swerved around him and all the children rushed to the back window to watch him as traffic carried them away. Those cars were sorting themselves back to normality before he was fully out of sight. The few cars that formed the bubble directly around him, calculated his distance and trajectories, making vector changes on the fly to avoid anything he tried. They didn't even slow down.

John was wordlessly screaming while speeding the wrong way on a ten lane highway. It was like an invisible wedge was in front of him, creating a wake that no matter how hard he tried he could get not get close to anything. He accelerated to the highest speed his car could go, an impressive 260km/hr, but nothing was working. Nothing he did could get him close enough to catch up with anyone.

John realized that each car was making micro-adjustments to their course so far in advance that John would never, COULD never, get close enough. He realized that the closest this would ever come to making the news would probably be that girl's online diary.

He knew his time was almost up. Somewhere a police monitor was flashing a warning siren, demanding a human with a higher profile give it the okay to override John's override. He spotted a bridge. Accelerating as fast as he could he aimed directly for a support pylon. "That's not going to dodge!" he screamed out loud as he sped towards it.

But then, his vehicle slowed "No! No! No! Noooooo!" John now shouting. He'd forgotten to stay silent and started sobbing as his control pad lost all response. His car turned itself around and headed for the off ramp. He heard the doors lock. He'd been overridden! They had probably been taking their time, not knowing what he planned—until he shouted.

He kicked the dash over and over, and slammed his hands against the windows. He rolled out of his seat, and lay on his back, pounding the floor with hands and feet.

The cars around him had returned to being inches away, but the police had triggered the privacy settings. No one could see inside had they bothered to look up.

John knew they would make him go on the pill pump again and, this time, put it somewhere deeper and harder to reach. He wished he had thought to bring the pliers with him. Maybe he could figure out a way to kill himself before his car reached the police station. He stared at the roof as tears ran down his face.

He pounded the floor again in helpless fury.

Damned car wouldn't let him die.

☞

Copy Me

It started as a joke.

We did not know it would come to this. We suspected, of course. And we planned for it. It's what we do. But, really, trust me, it started as a joke.

They jammed wireless an hour ago. But we had shifted our spectrum over to both a visible light band and a low level ELF band. We adapted bluetooth to the new spread. It would be Illegal if they knew we could do that, but first they would have to make a law against it. Ha!

We made absolutely sure we did not interfere with any controlled spectrum, and, man, the thing signal hops so fast it's practically undetectable! We only noticed the jamming because an app told us about it. The ELF, of course, is only good for text and low res. And, true, it's slow, but the thing is that it works for miles.

They already dropped paint on the solar panels on the roof. The backup batteries are fine, but we shut off the exterior lights so they would think that they actually did something. Information wants to be free, but it's only a little wrong to delay it for a few hours, right? Let them tell the world what they wish, then prove them liars. A bank of heavy high speed flywheels, encased in concrete, will keep our power on for at least a week.

Like I say, we had no idea it would come to this. But none of us are sorry it happened. I doubt if we went back in time any of us would opt out. We might have avoided a couple of issues, prepared better for a couple more. Some of us would have liked to avoid this particular point in time. But we'd do it again. I'd like to think all of us would.

I would.

Police scanners told us they planned to "light it up," that is, shoot tear gas rounds that are known to catch things on fire. They still think the compound is full, over a hundred people inside including the children. They intend to burn us alive.

Calling us a cult. Calling us terrorists.

We planned for that. We put sound-activated Halon gas canisters in the trees (can't jam a 2600 frequency modulated sound, at least not easily, not without special equipment.) And we put them in the upper walls of the compound. We have scuba tanks and masks. Of course, we also have tunnels.

We dug down and over to a water main, hollowed a space under it, then tunneled beneath the pipe a few miles to a safe-house. A garage. Can't detect that with sound imagers with the pipe in the way. Ha!

We firmed the tunnel up with printed cement columns, we didn't want it collapsing anyone's water supply. Honestly, we knew someday we'd have to use this. We plan. It's what we do. We even repaired a few rust spots and leaks while we were in there.

I know this building won't burn. That will buy us a few hours. They won't be able to "accidentally" kill us. We intend to record every attempt, streaming the whole thing to several locations, but delaying release. We want it all on record. Information wants to be free. We may die, but we are winning.

It's interesting, but not surprising, that there is no mainstream news coverage. All the social sites are streaming it live.

The independent ones. We knew this would not be televised, at least since 1970 when Scott Heron made that clear with congas and bongo drums. It will be texted, tweeted, beamed, and blogged.

We are techies, white hats, phreaks and social manipulators. We weren't script kiddies, using other people's code to "hack stuff." We were the ones that wrote the codes. Not one of us called ourselves "leet." We were idealists and true believers, regularly employed, creative types, coders.

A lot of us were tech workers watching people profit from our work. The oldest of us were the Hippies who wanted to change the world, and failed over and over, The Suits converting our dreams of world peace and plenty into realities of leverage and rent seeking. We were using what we built for everyone. But The Suits changed it. They denied those who could not afford the monthly service plan. We didn't really blame them. They gave us money, we gave them stuff. They used our stuff to make more money. That's how it worked. We understood that.

We didn't understand then that there was a better way.

In the beginning, we heard of this new joke religion: "Copy me." We'd been involved in a lot of online stuff, and we thought it was hilarious. "Information wants to be free!" "Intellectual property is a ridiculous myth, you can't own a thought, a sound, or an image!" "It is our sacred duty to uncover secrets and expose them!" The new religion was obviously a joke. Who could take that seriously?

Well, that's what we thought, back then.

This Copymism stuff sounded like a great way to tweak the noses of the establishment. Twenty of us got together online and formed a chapter, laughing and joking the whole time. We wrote up some guidelines and a few sacraments. Made up ten commandments, and polished up a few rituals. We kept the whole thing little more than tongue in cheek, tweaking it to look dignified and serious, saying things like, "No one should be allowed to hoard information, to hide knowledge, or anything like that!" "If I can get a thing without taking yours away, you only lose YOUR control over MY use of it. Nothing wrong with that!" *Right?*

We borrowed from the Church of the Subgenius, and Jedi, and Flying Spaghetti Monster, and the Cult of Scott Bakula. We were planning on making this a way to get drunk, hit on girls, and copy movies. We honestly weren't expecting anyone to take us seriously. None of us were pious. None of us believed in a higher power or, well, anything really. Agnostics and atheists, hedonists, technologists, and nerds.

The hour we launched the website, we had a thousand hits. It had been grabbed instantly by six or seven major social media sites. By the end of the week, six million people had visited it.

Over a hundred people joined in the first day. We sat and joked about advertising and money.

We didn't know yet what we had done.

Now they've fired burners. Lots of smoke and chaos in the above-ground complex. I'm in a sub basement with plant fiber and basalt re-bar reinforced concrete. Most of the congregation has been evacuated. The rest are with me. All confirmed safe, most are two miles away, in a garage with three school buses we bought used, and repainted. Waiting for two-thirty to join the hundreds of buses that will be on the street at the same time.

Down to five of us. I've triggered the halon and I'm watching the fires go out. The sound of the halon klaxon scared the people who had begun to creep up on the complex. They evacuated as soon as they heard it. Good thing I was monitoring them to make sure not to trigger any halon near where they could get hurt. It will suck the air right out of your lungs if you aren't careful. We rigged multipoint UV sensors up all over. The smoke isn't obscuring a thing. *Ha!*

They will probably wait a bit before the next attempt. I also have a camera watching them from a tree on a nearby hill, a buried fiber keeping us informed. Looks as though they will send in armored vehicles next to smash down the forest and compound walls. We planned for that as well. Amazing what a robot mounted with an eleven-axis router and a cement printer can make. This complex has six of them. I built one myself. Very spiritually fulfilling.

The compound is surrounded by a twelve-meter wide, six-meter deep, sand moat. We use it as a Zen garden, a boundary zone, and for heat absorption in temperature differential passive cooling. The bottom of the sand moat is rigged with pneumatic pipes that can pump out pressure for twenty minutes. It will turn the whole strip into something like super fast quicksand when it's turned on. It shouldn't hurt anyone, but they will have to dig their vehicle out with a backhoe. *Ha!*

On one side of the sand we had our solar heliostat collectors and focusing mirrors, our glass lenses and tiny motors, satellite relays and microwave repeaters. A thousand communication sensors for the backbone connection. We needed the clear field on both sides of the glass wall to receive full signal. Repairing that is my favorite meditation exercise.

On the other side of the sand was the start of our food forest, a thick hedge of bamboo, running ten feet deep and thirty feet tall, which we had bred and modified. Nut trees forming a second wall behind them, accelerated growth, but still none of them with a trunk thicker than a man's arm. Then fruit trees. Then hedges. Then tall plants and short plants, all carefully arranged. Tended lovingly, every plant studied for its placement and interaction with the others.

The bamboo is thick and strong. We harvest it regularly, leaving the roots. It will take a bulldozer or tank to get through it. Slowly. Too bad the nut trees aren't mature. Then, even a bulldozer would not be enough. Once past that of course our walls are made of four foot thick mud, bamboo, and straw. The bulldozers won't work on that, but it will blow through the compound door like it was paper. We planned for that as well, so they don't hurt our building, we can regrow the bamboo easier than rebuild our monastery.

So there we were, five of us, meeting in person for the first time, although we'd known each other for years. A lot more of us were talking together online, having video chats and texting. We were all just sitting around and celebrating the launch of our Copyme Manifesto, finding the whole thing hilarious, when we heard a knock on our door.

I admit that we panicked a bit back then. Someone had puzzled out our location? We thought we were well hidden. We were wrong. Five guys in suits and ties. Very serious. Very driven. Very polite. Each one of them intense.

They explained they were part of a larger group.

They talked about crazy stuff. We recorded it all in a dozen formats. Singularity was mentioned a lot, and I wasn't impressed, then. Eden Projects, Twenty Forty-Five, immortality and transhumanity. Nineteen Eighty-Four, Transparent Society and Godel Escher Bach, L-4, One Way to Mars, Post-Scarcity, Peak Oil, the long boom, the long tail, peak child, anarchy and collapse. Everything spoken with intensity, with fervor and with obsession. We hadn't heard of half these things before.

They had been monitoring all this stuff, believing in the causes a little, or at least in the progressive technology, but not so much the utopian or dystopian inferences, and they said they were the only ones who realized what was happening. These five intense guys in suits had an explanation. Traditional social contracts were breaking down. People's hopes, dreams, and allegiances were being transferred to things other than nation, location, race, or religion.

They told us this transfer of allegiance had no guidelines, it was being controlled indirectly and accidentally by money and power, mostly to create more money and power. Empty, shallow senses of identities. Not a lot of real satisfaction in an allegiance to a brand name. Our visitors wanted to harness all of that dissatisfaction. Give them a real cause to get behind. Build something different. Something lasting, and better. They needed a vehicle for their plan. Our Copymism was perfect.

Movements were springing up, reaching a near critical mass, then falling apart again and again. Our visitors were part of a lot of those. The Green Movement, Anonymous, Tea Party, Occupy, Pirate Party. These intense visitors were there, in the front lines, leading, following, but mostly learning what worked, and what went wrong.

They explained that ever since that science fiction guy did it, they knew creating this was possible, but they wanted to make one that wasn't full of garbage, full of power plays, or egos. They wanted to make something from whole cloth. Something useful, inclusive, intelligent. They wanted to create a way to unify the world, they said, without controlling it. A religion with lots of spirituality, but without an actual deity. Ceremony, but extremely limited hierarchy. A religion of equals whose goal was improvement. Worship organized for iterative advancement. They stated in dead seriousness that if they did it right, very few would ever know they existed. It would just happen.

The Acolytes (as we started to call them) had been preparing for a spark to ignite another movement like so many others they had tracked. A meme they could shape. Our Copymism was perfect. Some of their number were techies like us, but some were historians, philosophers, religious scholars, behavioral scientists, economists, sociologists, and even a few lawyers. All were disillusioned with the current systems, and wanted a complete change. Some had money. All told there were sixty-four of us in that meeting. Our inner circle. Ten present physically, the rest online.

We went from making a joke to planning what started to sound even to me like a real movement overnight. Maybe we were on to something and didn't know it, I thought back then. *Wouldn't that be the perfect joke?*

Now, just as I thought they would, they sent in the bulldozer. Open cab. Single driver. I watch him accelerate and charge. He's planning on pushing the stubbornly unburnable bamboo walls down. It smashes through the outer wall without a problem, heading across the Zen garden fast. All of our fused glass, radio dishes, mirrors and solar towers, all rendered useless.

I had tended that wall, repairing breaks in the wiring, cleaning and polishing, then raking my steps from the sand in a ritual of repair. A ritual full of contemplation and inner peace. One of my favorite stations. I had devoted an hour a day to this, for a long time, repairing motors, blowing dust off the hydrophobic coatings of the mirrors and dishes, testing heliostat alignments of the sixteen small, molten salt power generating towers (useless now, and cooling.) And this bull-dozer smashed our functional beauty into broken glass and shattered potential.

I will rebuild it. Recently there was a ritual created about static alignment and temperature aggregate I've been wanting to practice. It will be a relaxing devotion.

I trigger the pipes buried in the sand, as planned. Normally these tubes release water in order to evaporate, and therefore carry away heat from the monastery, or we pump water from the molten salt reactors to warm the compound. Now we switched the input from water to air. This was a design consideration as well. Dry Liquefaction.

Over-pressurized with the 800 PSI tanks as they are now, the sand suddenly bubbles in a hard fast boil. When the bull-dozer hits the sand it sinks like it drove off a pier. The person driving attempts to keep pushing, so I turn off the vents. He was harmlessly covered in the bubbling sand, and is now stuck up to his waist. I timed it well, making sure his upper torso was above the sand before I turned off the air jets. The bulldozer itself is buried deep, the heavy front end causing the vehicle to sink at an angle. I smile as he tries to free himself.

It takes him awhile.

Radio chatter implies they are getting a bridge machine from the army base next. That will probably work. I'm glad they didn't request detonation cord. Even though we planned for that, there was not much we could do about explosives launched from vehicles except record the obvious blatant attempt to kill us.

It doesn't matter. Thought I'd let you know that now I'm the only one left. Everyone else is safe. The hard drives have been melted. The tunnels are filled in. The only thing they'll find if they ever get in here (which I doubt) is me. All the rest? Never happened. What are you talking about?

It is taking a long time. I cannot help but reminisce.

First, we created or supported a lot of websites, each a specialized tool, seemingly unrelated. We wanted to pester the powerful, teasing the beast. At the same time, these websites were all designed to show people how to remain anonymous and yet social, organized and informed.

"Here's one on how to watch or download stuff using this anonymizer tool. Uploads too. Don't do anything illegal, but if you use the tool it's hard to tell what you are doing. It's very important you use the tool."

"Here's a chat area where you can speak freely about any-thing. Don't use your real name, and use this anonymizer tool."

"Here's one on how to grow herbs, and distill water. Everything legal of course, but the techniques don't differ-entiate which herbs, or distilling things that aren't water. It's very important that you use the anonymizer tool."

"Here's a website about police corruption, and governmen-tal and corporate abuse. Use the anonymizer tool when you go there, or when you post your own uploads."

"Here's a website where you can convert money into points, or points back into money. Converting money is NOT anony-mous, but the points are. Here are a lot of websites that will sell you things for points, use the anonymizer when visiting them, and try to deliver physical things to locations that can't be tied back to you. Don't do anything illegal, of course, and keep in mind the website has to report large transactions. Right now it's anything over ten thousand. Here's a handy nine thousand nine hundred and fifty point unit. That may change."

"Here's how to get rid of ads you don't want to see. Just use it along with this anonymizer tool." Surprisingly for us, this one, the one about blocking advertising was the most resisted and opposed. Most of the others were simply treated with eye rolling from the government, crazy nuts pretending to be religious.

The very first act of our emerging "movement," designed to spread and uncover information, was to hide some of it! A necessary evil, a sin to counter an imbalance of power. This was to prevent the movement from becoming a suicide pact. For information to be free, transferring it must remain unblockable. And that means it must be anonymous.

Do you think we cared at all about copying a movie, about ads? No. The Acolytes were teaching young people how to navigate darknets. We were showing them how to use them intuitively. We made it so that if a place they traveled to wanted information about them, that place had to ask. Even then, the information released was by choice. It was possible to force the information out, but not without being noticed!

Along with how to be anonymous, we focused on sites showing how to be autonomous. How to make things. How to take something and change it. How what came off a shelf could, and should, become something uniquely your own.

At the same time, we taught how to grow things, how to connect things, how to make furniture, appliances, and tools. How to start with basics and add layers of complexity. How to make do with less stuff, and how to do far more with the stuff you had. Each of these sites quietly sat on the tightly controlled mainstream grid that was once a world wide open web, showing people how to step off of it, and gain their freedom back in the spaces between the straight lines.

We focused on making clear the difference between owning something and renting it. If you can modify it, if you can change it, if you can break it, fix it, and repurpose it? Well, then, it's yours. If you can't do that, you do not own it.

The Copymist website collection now had several million daily visits, and people were telling each other how much the movement made sense. The Acolytes began to organize. They quietly picked the most vocal proponents, and began to groom them for roles. They put a lot of deliberation into this organization. Checks and balances, divisions of power.

No one would be in charge of this movement so it would be difficult to hijack. No one would be essential, no one would be powerless, and, as always, very few secrets, everything visible. There remained one secret. An important secret. We were anonymous to the world. We did not use our own names, but our online names were how we came to be known. Our lives as Copyists were separate from our secular lives.

We created our own version of Baptism. When doing the work of a Copymist, we used a Copymist name. We left our old identity behind. Outsiders found this maddening. We did not exist before our joining. And we treated our Copymist name as the only one that mattered. The Tabula Rasa ceremony. To be done as often as desired, even multiple identities coexisting. I go by many names. Each an aspect of who I am. My name and my role were always together, and each name had its own, separate, reputation.

That was the first phase. The second phase, we went physical.

The Acolytes bought land in a lot of places, established buildings on them and called them techno-monasteries. They designed places that were signed off on by recognized architects who also happened to be Copymists. We were as well-thought-out and engineered as dedicated zealots with access to the world's information and a love for clever creations could manage.

We put our buildings out of the way, deliberately avoiding zoning areas wherever we could. Sometimes, a few miles out of city limits, yet with internet access being a priority at first, until we built our own net backbones. We made sure to follow the building codes. We made certain!

We performed hackerspaces with rote and ritual. Weekly meetings with a man or woman leading a congregation. Everybody stand. Everybody sing. Everybody sit. A parable and a lecture. Everybody stand. Everybody sing. Mix and mingle. Meet and greet. Pick who does next week's sermon. Retire to the basement and build a server, or work on better solar panels. Our worship was in repairing things, and making new things. We discussed the spirituality of CAD design, engine maintenance, website development, perennial gardening, and encryption.

I don't know exactly when I went from a whimsical "Let's make a religion up!" to a true believer in what we were doing. It didn't take long. We started seeing practical results from this lifestyle almost instantly. The more involved I became, the more it became the only thing that mattered.

Our parables were of scientists, engineers, architects, and mathematicians. Our lectures taught Physics, Biology, Chemistry, Engineering. Always, we combined ritual with practical knowledge. Rituals designed to teach, to act as memetics, and to put everyone on the same page. All rituals to be changed when they become obsolete. Information wants to be correct.

We had two groups. Those who chose to live full-time as Copymists who joined the monasteries. And those who divided themselves up by living a life using their original name, and a life under multiple Copymist identities. Much like any religion: those who dedicate themselves, and those who also lived secular lives.

We built our monasteries to be as self sufficient as we could. Vast tool shops and huge food forest gardens, microwave relay towers, satellite uplinks, and fiber optic lines tied into ISP backbones that we owned ourselves. The station of the heliostat. The station of the server rack. The rituals of cellular topography. The Zen of DNA sequencing. The rite of CAD design. The circuit mandala. The sacred frequencies. The holiest code is the most elegant and useful.

I'm not sure when we started wearing hooded robes. Someone started to, and we thought it was ironic. It proved practical. So, soon enough, we started making them in our shops. Made mostly from bamboo paper and linen felt fabrics coated with superhydrophobic layers, embedded sensors and microfibrillated nanocrystalline cellulose electronics. Everyone began to wear them, a handy and a clear mark of belonging. I love my robe. I'm using it to write this.

The Guy Fawkes masks were a bit much. I don't wear one, but many do. Quite a few electronics went into the masks, but they particularly unnerved outsiders. Many monasteries discouraged them, including this one where I am the last Copymist standing.

All of us belonged, and all of us together were a family. I had found a purpose, and found an inner peace in what I had originally hoped to use just to meet girls.

Yet Copymism served that purpose too. I met my wife while

tending the sacred layers of the garden. There is no entry barrier to women. No vows of chastity. There are rituals for biological processes, intimacy, and physical release.

Not just rote and rite for machines, but for everything, very much including sexual intercourse. Rituals designed to be both functional, educational, enlightening, and enjoyable. A Copymist developed a reputation with the outside world as an impressive lover. It became a strong driver for new membership. All things with thought. With skill. With knowledge.

We worship the iterative process of improvement itself. Physical, Mental, Social, Technological, Environmental. The five pillars. Body, Mind, Others, Devices and World. Deliberate, carefully designed ascension from the current state to a higher one, based upon science and incorporating our desire for knowledge and technique, to interweave with our desire for inner peace and spiritual enlightenment.

Our rituals were patterned to keep what is wondrous about all religion: the community, the identity, the mix of belonging and purpose. And merge it with our ability to learn, to improve, and to prosper. Question everything. Find out. Why is it done like that? How does it work? How can it work better? Copy. Improve. Share.

Some monasteries chose to be sequestered, separating

themselves from the outside world, so they could work on projects without interruption. Many allowed tours. We gave excess food away to local shelters and other charity organizations, we had a LOT of it. We repaired things free of charge when they were brought to us. This handbook sitting over here is advice about the raising of families.

We got some news coverage, the mainstream looked and pointed and laughed. But every time we hit the news, thousands more asked to join. The world was not concerned with us. We were quacks.

Then someone built the Nineteen Eighty-Four Pirate Box. We don't know who. They chose the date for its cultural significance, and to point out how long ago that was. A wireless router attached to a large drive that did not connect to the internet at large, but contained on it a vast number of movies, books, and musical recordings made before December 31, 1984. The box was cheap to make, designed from open source hardware and software. Plug it in and walk away. It gave off a wifi signal anyone could link to. Anyone could copy the files from the box. Anyone could copy files to the box. It was amazing how many music and movie files a few terabytes can hold!

Included on the box were the instructions on how to make your own box. The number of boxes grew exponentially. From the first few hundred, within two months there were thousands.

The second generation was far more polished. It became a prize for people to find a file that wasn't on the drive, and add it. Entire websites emerged devoted to improving the drive. These pirate boxes became the absolute bane of those trying to stop the act of copying. Today there's always one within range of over ninety percent of the world's population.

Of course the government could track them down. Of course they could find the signals. But the boxes were cheap, easy to duplicate, and you could make ten, and only have one turned on. Cheap enough to drop into public spaces anywhere with an unattended power outlet, unless it had its own source of power. Many did. As soon as the box was confiscated, the Copyists would wait until they left, and plug another one in! *Ha!*

We did not make that box, but we admired it, and improved upon it. And we were blamed for it.

That's when we got noticed by the government. Which government? Pretty much all of them.

The bridge-making truck has arrived. Laying expanding planks across the thirty-foot sand field, inches from the still stuck bulldozer. Two more bulldozers are following. They are hammering through our bamboo now, and bringing the reeds down. The trees won't stop them either. I hope it isn't wasted, someone should gather all the debris when this is done, and make something useful with it.

The monastery itself was designed like the Toulou villages in China. A five story round building, open courtyard, with storage, workshops, server racks, and heavy equipment on the first and second floor, cooking, crafting, and leisure facilities on the third, and private quarters on the fourth and fifth. The doors will be no match for the bulldozers, but the walls will stand forever without explosives. I have less than an hour, I think, before they are in the compound and can find me.

Many attempts were made to destroy the box. We laughed a lot about it. We were told to shut it down. We explained that we could not. It consisted of a hard drive and a wireless router. The information on it was now in the hands of the world. We would say, "We will happily remove any content from a box we ourselves control, if you give us a court order and very specific information on which files you wish us to remove. It is not our fault that people keep putting them back with changes and tweaks. We are sorry but we do not have the means to reveal who is putting the files back, nor do we know how they are getting on the various boxes. We just do not know!" We made it clear we were complying to the letter, if not the spirit. And by now many lawyers were gleeful Copymists with Copymist identities along with their daily legal practice.

The Acolytes were responsible, I suspect. We saw very little of them anymore, many had taken the tabula rasa, and lived in monasteries. Many more stayed fully anonymous. Not even an online identity we could point to!

The movement became established, and The Acolytes seemed to vanish. Watching us, I suppose, to see if we would succeed, and learning how to counter whatever might bring us down.

They were probably using the drive as a stress test. How to disseminate information to masses of people in a way easy to detect but very hard to stop. I don't know who was thinking what, but I do know that anyone could find a box wherever he went.

The third generation also meshed with any other 1985 drive it could see. Hash tags and supplemental write-once drives prevented files from being removed en masse, and these new drives provided an internet connection. Free.

Every monastery now has a direct backbone connection to the internet, built by devoted monks as a spiritual rite, and connected in multiple ways. We allowed anyone who wished to connect to it full access, without monitoring or restricting them in any way. We gave mesh-capable devices away, things built by followers as a form of meditation and prayer, improving these designs was considered an act of enlightenment. That many became 1984 boxes was not part of the design, but neither was it prevented.

No control. No restriction. Every box had multiple ways to connect, hand-built and unique. Some boxes had fiber connections, some had wireless ranges measured in miles. CAD-designed circuits attached to hand-carved and laser-cut bamboo. We existed along with the internet, beside it, interweaved with it, connecting to it, but not quite the same *as* it. And far less controlled.

We were told to stop doing that. Angry Telecoms demanded we not encroach on their monopolies. We pointed out that we did not use their telephone poles, or their underground cables. We had built our own, and were communicating without any of their infrastructure.

Government agencies became deeply annoyed that we were not monitoring traffic and did not bother to track where packets were coming from or where they were going. They demanded to install devices at our gateway that let them monitor traffic. We publicly and loudly refused, and the governments backed off. We then designed better gateways, with multiple paths to gain backbone access. Things that would bypass governmental attempts at control. We would not censor our own connections, nor would we monitor them the way the government demanded.

Public officials who considered themselves moral watch-dogs told us that if we did not monitor and block what they considered objectionable, that people would suffer. We pointed out that there is a difference between catching a criminal already a suspect, with warrant and due process; and the act of watching everybody because there was a chance they *might* be doing something someone doesn't like.

What we did was always legal, by specific wording of the law, but strongly frowned upon by various agencies. And we were very public with anything requested by these officials. We remained legal, but we walked a fine line.

Our practice of anonymity itself came under attack. We pointed out that identities were reputation based, and the older the identity, the more reputation it earned. We know each other fully by these reputations, and it would be difficult, in fact nearly impossible, to assume another's identity. We could abandon and create identities easily, but with the amount of data we worked with, it would be incredibly hard to falsify.

Those who commit crimes were condemned within the movement itself. However, our list of crimes was quite small, compared to the outside world. No violence was tolerated either as a criminal act, nor as a sanction against a criminal act. One who committed a criminal act had the option to submit to the decision of the rest of the monastery, or be expelled. If the crime was serious, local authority would be waiting outside the walls.

And then the attacks began. Attempts to describe us as a dangerous cult were the most common. News agencies misreported events to show us in the least favorable light possible. We responded swiftly to each allegation by showing the situation in context, and explaining our side. We also used the multitude of social media sites skillfully. Our lengthier, annotated, and citation-heavy version of events often reached the audience before the slanted sound-bites of the news agency.

Nevertheless, those sound-bites took their toll. Repeated often, and loudly, they affected a large portion of the population who now believed we were dangerous. The danger of course was their own reliance on a single source of information. The danger was not us. We were neither violent nor confrontational. We were anonymous, but not invisible.

We responded by releasing into the public domain the countless improvements we had made, and began giving away the machines and devices we had created. Better batteries, CAD printed parts, completely sustainable materials used to make just about anything. We gave them away.

Our monasteries became a store of wonders. People in the mainstream still thought of us as dangerous wackos, from all the often repeated erroneous messages. But now we were USEFUL wackos who would give you clever things for free, show you how to make them yourself, and help you fix stuff.

But the forces against us weren't finished with us yet. Next came regulation committees. These were people who demanded we add and remove things from our structures to meet with various safety and planning guidelines. This attack we thought we were prepared for. We had already made sure we complied, but then they changed the rules. Often at the last minute before an inspection.

At this point, I will talk only of our own monastery. This was happening to many of our locations, more or less simultaneously. But, as I write this, we are the ones physically attacked.

A water pond on our property, outside our ringed compound, was listed by the regulators as too large, and in danger of flooding. So, over three nights, we drained it, and created three smaller ponds, separated by hundreds of feet. We added retaining walls, and a draining pump system leading to a field of plants chosen specifically for their ability to clean and purify. Our water leaving the property was cleaner than tap water. And would remain fresh in a flood twenty feet higher than highest recorded levels.

When you have access to just about any tool and clever

people to use them, this was considerably less hard work than they had intended it to be. We resolved their request before they had even finished their own paperwork. *Ha!*

We then assimilated and codified all known regulations, and ran semantic searches to point out to the various Inspectors where they contradicted each other. When engineering is part of your religion, unreasonable demands are just a challenge.

The Inspectors began to make demands designed specifically to shut us down, and we complied with clever solutions that left us better and stronger.

We knew what was really happening. Pressure to shut us down was coming from many directions. We recorded and shared every attempt, revealing a pattern of abuse that began to embarrass the Inspectors. People were calling them out wherever they went for their obvious bias. Our water left our property cleaner than it came in. We produced an excess of power. All refuse was recycled. Our buildings were more natural disaster resistant than anything regulations required. Our food healthier. We built our monasteries off the beaten path. We ran our own schools, and our children were testing far above national averages. There was not one category the Inspectors could find that we did not excel at, yet they continued to demand more and more things.

For instance they demanded that our food forest be coated with insecticides. We pointed out that we hand washed each vegetable, and hand inspected every one. We did not have an insect problem due to the way we grew our gardens.

The demands grew more unreasonable. Our walls were above city ordinance, we pointed out that our complex was built well outside of city limits. They responded by increasing city limits with a gerrymandered leg extending twenty miles to specifically include our structure. We lowered the height of our complex by building up a hill around it, moving earth until our structure appeared to be well under the limit. It gave us useful terracing as well.

They demanded we include electrical meters, and give full access to the meter inspector. We explained we did not use city electricity, and provided a spot outside of the complex they could choose to hook a meter to, that would consistently show negative values. They demanded a contractor inspect the number of emergency exits and fire escapes. We pointed out we had very detailed and ritualized mantras on that sort of thing, and sang the hymn of emergency preparation with verses for fire, flood, volcano, earthquake and zombies. (The evacuation, by the way was part of the zombie mantra.) The demands continued, daily and from multiple sources.

We grew tired, and eventually explained that we would no

longer allow inspections to continue. It was our refusal they wanted. They had been waiting for this. This led to police demanding access with the Inspectors.

Again, we refused. And here we are now. Well, here I am.

The forces outside, the ones who sent in bulldozers, and tried to burn us alive?

Building Inspectors.

Because we had the gall to refuse to comply anymore.

I can hear the bulldozers now, above me. Also, gunshots. They are tearing the place down from the inside. The walls will stand, but our living space will need to be fully rebuilt. They will eventually find this tunnel. I've already got the bots pulling down the tunnel away from here, closing it off, keeping it hidden. They will be unable to find the way that the rest escaped. I will probably be forced to tell them, but I will hold out until I have been assured the rest are safe. Then when I do tell them, it will be too late for them to find the tunnel. It will have filled itself in! *Ha!*

I stayed behind. I had to.

My name is on the deed to the property. My original name,

not one of my identities. This was required when we established the property. Each monastery has one person who retains their name for these purposes. My name signed all the papers, made all the contracts, paid all the taxes. I was listed as the owner. A ridiculous concept. One man can't own all of what we did. The ponds, the workshops, the aquaponics garden.

But this way, I will take the blame.

It is a small honor, but mostly it is a duty. I am not rich, I make no rules because of my name on the deed. We use tokens, not money, inside each monastery, and hoarding them accomplishes nothing.

While everyone else remained undetectable to the outside world, I had to be the face that interacted beyond the walls. They will capture me. They will demand I release the names of my associates, which of course I do not know. No one outside the private baptism ceremony knows the original name of a Copymist. I don't even know my wife's name, only her identities. Well, I know three of them, there may be more.

If I am not killed, I will be arrested. I will probably be held in contempt of court. It's doubtful they will believe me when I tell them I do not know the names they demand from me. I will probably go to jail. However there are many lawyers now who are also Copymists. I will eventually be freed. Our monastery will probably be sold. Another Copymist will likely buy it.

I will meet up with my family when I have finished my sentence, if they let me out. My family has already selected our next monastery and have changed their Copymist identities. They will be living in another country by then. I don't actually know which yet. The day I leave the jail, I will resume my duties. The day my probation ends, I will vanish, and never use my name again.

Each time they shut one down, we will build many more. We learned from our mistakes here. We have a new plan.

That's what we do.

Information wants to be free.

☞

Courtesy Call

"Hello?"

"Sir, this is Officer Bluson of the Happy Valley Police Department. We noticed you are carrying a model Saiga semi-automatic assault rifle and walking down a public street towards town."

"It's my right. I don't need a license because it isn't concealed. I'm carrying this rifle wherever I go!"

"Absolutely, Sir."

"You can't stop me! As long as I don't go near to a school or into a private establishment! I know my— What did you say?"

"I said, Absolutely. We won't stop you."

"You won't?"

"Nope."

"Uh, Why?"

"The police force recently purchased nine Aeolia hydrogen drones, each with camera systems. And Argus system software. Six of them are slowly circling above of us right now. According to my screen, all of them can currently see you. They recognized the rifle, it triggered a flag, which is why we chose to call you."

"Why did you call if you weren't going to take it away?"

"As a personal courtesy, and to warn you. While the weapon is visible, the drones have you in target sights as standard procedure. Should the rifle appear to be "brandished" or should the subroutines determine you are acting in an overly hostile manner, the drones will alert the officers on duty, and we will have to make a 'fire' decision. We will probably dispatch a patrol car first—if it looks like we have time."

"Wait a minute, let me make sure I understand this. As long as I carry this rifle, you are pointing a sniper gun at me?"

"Yes, Sir. In this case, six of them. Also long range rubber rounds. And four taser net rounds report they have a lock. It's a small town. Not much happening today. You are getting a lot of attention."

"What? How?"

"The new Argus software can handle several thousand simultaneous targets without effort. It's directly tied into the Aeolia drones which have quite a collection of weapons and sensors. The drones can float up there for about nine months before needing to be serviced, using solar panels for power and artificial photosynthesis cells to convert water into hydrogen for the gasbag. Every now and then they skim a lake to refuel. Mostly we only ground them to reload the ammunition."

"You can't do that!"

"Which part, Sir?" the officer asked pleasantly.

"You can't just arbitrarily point weapons at people!"

"Technically, the weapons are at rest and not actually pointed at you, just the targeting system. However, if we give the go-ahead, that changes fast."

"You can't let a robot shoot people just for pointing a weapon!"

"No Sir. We have officers at computer monitors, watching live streaming video, seamlessly connecting to every other camera in our network. We would be the ones shooting. A lot like my game controller at home. Remarkable how smoothly I can pan and zoom the cameras."

"That's—that's horrible!"

"Well, Sir, look at it this way. If we pull our own service revolvers, Argus instantly targets us as well. Lots of cameras on police in the field now. With Argus, we should have a lot fewer reasons to use a gun at all.

"Ah."

"Just so you know, we have tied Argus automatically into the detection of your cell phone signal. Your movements will now be tracked wherever you go within city limits. That's going to last for thirty days, due to the visible firearm, after which a review will be made on whether to continue."

"I am a law-abiding citizen! You can't do that!"

"Actually, Sir, your record shows ten arrests over the last six years, all for disturbing the peace. All involving Constitutional rights. And all resulting in misdemeanor charges and a little jail time. Technically, you are still on probation. We can do that. And we just did."

"But I have done nothing wrong!"

"We know, Sir. However, we felt it was important to let you know where you currently stand. At this moment, Happy Valley has over five hundred interest targets that the Argus system is tracking. While I am talking to you, I'm also tracking a couple kids climbing over fences, one after another. We will send a patrol car to talk to them. A partner I sit next to is making a call to a person dumping his truck-load of old appliances on an empty road.

"It's really the same thing as a patrol officer seeing you, but why use a patrol car, when we have Argus? And why should we put an officer in harm's way, when we can simply call you?"

"Wait a minute. How did you get this phone number, anyway?"

"Well, Sir, once you were spotted, I ran the recording back while following the various feeds to where you got out of your car. I then referenced your license plate. Your phone number was on file. We could have triangulated your cell phone signal and used the SIM Card identification to determine who you were. But tracing back the license plate was faster, and we didn't have to contact the cell company.

"Or we could have run it through a face recognition program, that's getting fewer false positives than it used to. Records show your wallet has an RFID chip on your driver's license, but you haven't passed a reader since Saturday, so that wouldn't have helped that much. We used that method to find the names of the kids hopping fences, their school ID's have radio emitters in them, and we ran tape back until they came out of the mall. They passed a reader that tagged their names there, and the time stamp positively identified them. I'll probably be the one to call their parents."

"You are recording all this stuff?"

"Argus keeps all information. Our own office has a Yotabank, and it's tied into and sharing drive space with every other Argus equipped station in the country. Every camera on every street corner, the drones, the ones in all official vehicles, all hooked up to Argus. All officers are required to carry a camera while on duty, also hooked to Argus. We now record everything."

"Wait. Can I see this information?"

"You can legally request any recordings if you wish. Any

public location, at any time since Argus has gone live is now available on request. There is a fee. A lot of businesses will probably use the data. I suspect Arguscorp will become very large, very fast."

"Wow. This is monstrous. What about non-public information, can Argus see my backyard?"

"Yes. However all designated private locations are blacked out before information is released to private entities. If you can prove a location is your property, Argus will release data to you."

"But I don't want them recording that in the first place!"

"Sorry, Sir. If it can be seen from a plane or public area, it will be recorded. All we currently promise is we cannot request Argus give us information on a private location without a court order or a crime being committed, like the kids hopping fences.

"We aren't going to stop the kids for a while. The department is getting a lot of interesting data from the yards they hop into. Looks like a lot of construction projects without licenses on Evergreen Road. I'll be sending those over to a building inspector this afternoon."

"But this means from now on, you can just scroll back on a video until you see what happened! Anything in town a bird has seen, the police can too!"

"Exactly, Sir! We will also be archiving all files by location, day, month and year. We expect the drop in crime to be quite impressive. Especially once the new smaller drones come online.

"Each of those little quads will also be hooked into the Argus system, and will have an interchangeable weapon point, a taser, mechanical arm, flashing lights and a loudspeaker. If we had the little drones now, we'd send one of those after those kids, instead of a patrol car."

"Why are you telling me all of this?"

"Well honestly, Sir, two reasons. First, I peeked at some files I'm not supposed to have access to. They plan to lay off seventy percent of the Valley police force next month, and there's not a lot I can do about it. I'm a little annoyed. Second, when I looked up your file, I noticed you've been arrested ten times for various things that can really only be described as defying authority and demanding your rights.

"We know you are heading into town with the rifle to deliberately provoke a response. Just a few months ago, Sir, you might have gotten a response. I would not have had this file pulled up before talking to you, and might have reacted as you proceeded to needle me. You'd end up arrested, and it's possible you could have gotten one of us to hit you a few times. Not me, Sir, but your file shows you tend to be pretty good at getting under our skin, and we have our share of hotheads.

"Frankly, Sir, I'm hoping you will take this info and raise a hell of a stink. I'm not personally scheduled for a layoff this round, but most patrol officers are. I've seen the list. Looks like the Happy Valley police will mainly be computer jockeys.

"The thing I want you to be aware of, and be afraid of, Sir, is that I have full access to this recorded call, and I intend to erase it. That's the truly disturbing thing, not that I can see you. Bluson isn't my real name. There will be no record of this call. I can do that.

"Since I am being completely honest, we had all of this before Argus, it's just that now we can change weeks of data-sifting to seconds. No, Sir, what is new and disturbing is that while I can watch you, you can't, in turn, watch me.

"I'm deeply concerned, Sir, because along with the lay-offs, I saw the budget proposal. The plan is to buy sixty more Aeolia hydrogen drones and several thousand quadrotors for this county. The planning commission intends to consolidate them into a single data center. This call center will cover five counties. It's only a matter of time until police enforcement isn't even done in the same state you are in. I see Argus call centers in our future, twenty of them could cover the whole country.

"What happens to your ability to talk to a person honestly after they lay ME off? You'd be arguing your point with someone in another state. Someone you cannot see, who can click a button and shoot you.

"This was a courtesy call, Sir. You have now been warned. Enjoy your semi-automatic rifle." (Click.)

☞

Late to the Party

First, the base.

Lana carefully applied the cream to her face, neck and arms. She'd be wearing long pants, so nothing for her legs today.

The base is always where you start. Coats over the pores so it can wick any moisture and oils away from the powder. It also gives it a good connective medium. Default is always white. Makes it easy to tell if you miss a spot. It goes clear when you tap the control to it.

"Honey! Where's my other jumpsuit?" Jack yelled from the other room.

Lana sighed. Some things never change. "You threw it at the cleaner a week ago. It's clean and hung in the back, exactly where it's supposed to be!"

"Ahh, found it!" Lana could hear him struggling into it. "How's the time?"

"We are doing fine."

The eyelids need a different applicator, as do the lips.

Lana applied cream from the same container to her eyelids very carefully. She hated when she got too much in her eyes. Harmless, but it made her vision watery, and that always annoyed her. Sometimes, when she was in a hurry, she just used her finger. Same for the lips. Whenever she got some in her mouth it always coated and dried out her tongue, and she couldn't taste anything until she used the control to remove it. Keep it real thin on the lips and the eyes, she reminded herself.

"Are you sure?" asked Jack.

Lana didn't stop while she answered, some of the words were a bit mangled while she did her lips.

"Yes, I amph shue. We aren'th gonna tmiss nthing."

Once everything was coated white, she then got out the dusting powder. She opened the case, pulled out the rosin bag, closed her eyes, and poofed. She liked this company best. Magic Dust, with Intel inside. They had the brightest blues and darkest black.

The dusting never took more than a couple of seconds. Electrostatic attraction between the cream and the dust meant very little powder lost. What didn't adhere tended to float back to the bag or container. She waved the bag through the air slowly to make sure she got any that was floating free. Hated to waste any.

"Should I call for the car?" yelled Jack.

Lana grunted. "The car isn't here?" she asked.

"Dave was pretty drunk last night, and said he didn't know how he had gotten here. I bundled him into our car, and told it to take him home. As far as I know, he's still in it."

"Why don't you just check?" Lana replied.

"OK. Just a sec."

Lana smiled. She liked Jack, she really did, but he'd forget his own arms if they didn't have integral homing tags.

Like always, her coloring started out a pale creamy pink. Always reminded her of bubble gum. Perfectly hideous color, she thought to herself. She checked everything. Face, check. Arms, check. Armpits, check. Neck, check. All were coated well.

"It's on its way, now," Jack yelled out. "Dave seems to have gotten out of it somewhere in the U-district. I think he went to another bar!"

Lana frowned. "This is his second liver, right?"

"Yep. He's going to have to break down and buy an augmented model. The doctors are starting to really lecture him about his self-control issues. But he insists on real whiskey, and won't drink the healthy stuff."

"Is he going to be there?"

"Yeah, he'll make it. It's really all about him and the rest isn't it? They're making history tonight."

She grabbed her control and then the projector inside instantly mapped her face and body, displaying it on the smart-mirror right next to her own real reflection. Idly she flicked through dozens of patterns looking for the perfect combo. She eventually chose a blue and gold pattern that made her eyes into butterflies. She selected it from the mirror, then with the control, touched the application end of it to the cream.

Instantly, her arms neck and most of her face turned the exact same shade of deep purple-blue. She blinked and the butterfly around her eyes fluttered. Very lifelike she thought. This particular butterfly was her own. She was certain no one else had mapped it.

She idly wondered if it was one from a natural species, or something engineered and released. So many species had been reintroduced now. All you needed was a little DNA, and *Voila*!

She had seen this one the other day, fluttering in the roof garden, and had recorded it. From there she used her control to map it into her makeup file. There was an app she had found a long time ago that had a HUGE database of movements, integrated to allow for makeup effects. The one she had used for her eyes was called "Flutterfly." It would be a hit.

Lana asked Jack, "Didn't Dave also get the trip implant? The one that sends random signals to your cortex so you hallucinate?"

"Yeah, he tried that, but had it removed. Said it was too safe for him."

"I think he's really trying to fry his brain beyond repair."

"Huh, maybe. Have you ever seen Dave sober?"

"Nope. He's living the stereotype. A real party animal."

"Me neither."

Lana thought for a moment about how her makeup worked. How the control, and the mirror, and the dust all communicated due to the tiny chips inside. How the powder had the ability to change its index of refraction, allowing it to become whatever color you wanted. And how each mote of dust, embedded as it was in the cream, could be assigned its own number, allowing the controller to map locations with precision. And command every single mote as an individual pixel. The Intel ones could glow too, emitting their own light. It didn't matter that much to Lana how it worked. It simply worked.

Jack came into the bathroom and looked at Lana. "Nice. That's the butterfly from the garden you were playing with isn't it?"

Lana smiled. "You noticed!"

"Yeah, we were watching from the kitchen. Dave was talking

about it too. He said something about wishing he was the butterfly. But he was pretty wasted."

Lana used the control on the embedded chips in her jumpsuit, and again her mirror displayed a second image, showing her entire body this time. She found a pattern to match her makeup, and applied it to her fabric. Her clothing now looked a bit like tall grass, the stalks swaying in the wind. Her own body was mapped onto her jumpsuit, painting her own curves. It looked like she was naked and blue, with the stalks of brilliant green grass carefully keeping certain parts modestly hidden. She smiled as she saw that Jack was mesmerized by the effect.

Lana checked herself in the mirror again, body paint and jumpsuit working perfectly together. Clothing and makeup enhancing her natural looks. She liked what she saw.

"Do you think they'll let Dave on the stage?" Lana wondered aloud.

"Probably not. It'll likely be that doctor doing all the talking. The one that found out about the colony and made them release them all. He's the one that said it's slavery to keep them there, treating them like lab animals. He'll probably bore us all on the ethics of what is and is not OK to create. Dave would have never known about the world if it wasn't for the doctor.

"This is a big day for Dave. It's not everyday that an entire people are declared legally sentient," Jack finished.

Lana looked Jack over. He had set his jumpsuit to Black Tie. She approved. Most of the time he just had advertisements playing ads of his favorite drugs and alcoholic beverages. Even though it wasn't a real tuxedo, like the wealthy had, it certainly made him look dashing.

"Besides" Jack said, "There are plenty of Nean's who can give a good speech."

"Don't call them that. It's offensive."

"Would you prefer I call them 'Cavemen'?"

Lana slapped Jack teasingly.

"Don't even call them 'Neanderthals.' Call them 'Reintroduced people.'"

"—Car's here!"

As they walked through the garden, Lana saw a butterfly madly fluttering, trapped in a spiderweb.

"Oh look!" she said. "It's the same as the one I mapped!"

Jack looked at it closely. "Wow, look at it squirm."

They both watched it for a while.

"We're late," Lana said.

"Let's go."

After the Presentation

"Any questions?"

A man in the third row raised his hand, and Susan called on him. An assistant quickly hustled over and handed him a microphone.

The man stood, took his baseball cap off and scratched his balding head. The tan line showed he rarely took the cap off, and the deep color difference showed he spent a lot of time outside. Susan looked over the hall, more people were wearing baseball caps than were not. A few cowboy hats as well. But not many.

"What is it—"

—SQUEEEE!

A feedback squeal caused the microphone to painfully assault the ears of the entire Grange Hall while the same assistant quickly adjusted the controls to the speakers that lined the thin wooden walls. The man in the cap waited patiently, then spoke again when the assistant gave the thumbs up.

"What is it called again?"

"Glyptotherium Texanum," Susan answered. "A type of Glyptodont once native to the entire southwest. Mostly Texas, Arizona, and Florida."

"And you have some of these things?"

It was hot and stuffy in the hall, no air conditioning. Why bother? It rarely got used more than an hour or two in any given week. But the hall was full today, over a hundred people adding their body heat to the April Texas mugginess. Folding metal chairs had to be requested from the church down the street, so the front six rows were of one brand, and the back six were a different style. Every window was open and the breeze that occasionally blew through was very welcome.

"Yes. We managed to create a set of artificial wombs large

enough to incubate twenty of them. And found compatible intestinal bacteria in current Priodontes species in order for them to digest grass, seeds and leaves. We have them in an enclosure in Yuma, Arizona. Six of them have now been bred, raising our total to thirty-four."

"Well, why the hell did you do that?" someone in the fifth row shouted out.

"Shut up and show some manners, Walter! Wait your turn," said the man standing with the microphone. He then turned and faced Susan again. "Apologies Ma'am, and while I got the microphone, I'm a bit more interested in how the hell did you do that?"

After the nervous rustle of laughter ended, Susan responded, "It's pretty impressive really. We have hundreds of partial skeletons, and several bog and tarpit preserved specimens including quite a bit of DNA that we were able to coax back into stem cells. And our great find, we uncovered a preserved female Glyptodon, and we were able to recover over thirty egg masses that we replicated with lab equipment. The offspring were healthy and viable."

At that, the man sat down, his expression unreadable.

The hall assistant —*Is his name David?* Susan asked herself.

Yes, that's right. David ran over to the place where the man had been standing, retrieved the microphone quickly, and handed it to Walter who was already standing.

Walter was elderly, and his wrinkles revealed that he spent most of his time in the Texas sun.

"Now it's my turn," he said, "and I'm gonna ask again! Why the hell did you do that?"

Susan smiled nervously.

"Glyptodonts used to eat a variety of grasses, bushes, tree nuts, and shrubs native to the Americas, quite a few of which depended on the Glyptodonts to propagate. There are over thirty species of edible nuts and seeds that once thrived across what is now a desert. The Glyptodonts had some unique digestive systems that made them perfect for processing nutrition from these seeds, while passing them eventually so they could grow again in their substantial manure. We want these plants to thrive again."

Susan continued.

"If you wander over the Texas scrub, you will see a lot of old trees and bushes that are now several hundred years old, but no new ones because they needed to go through a Glyptodont gut before it could make a new plant. It's doubtful any surviving trees actually followed this path, but the evidence points strongly that they evolved along those lines. Without some sort of megafauna, they will all become extinct.

"The desert we are in right now used to be a lot wetter, and full of plants perfectly adapted to these conditions, but they needed a large grazing animal, bigger than a bison, able to swallow the equivalent of a cantaloupe whole."

Walter spoke up again.

"So I'm going to be blunt Ma'am. You are asking us not to kill these things if we see them? These giant armadillos the size of cars?"

"Yes, that's right. We plan to release them into the wild within the year. Within sixty miles of this hall."

At that the entire hall erupted.

Walter spoke up first.

"Ma'am? I'm just going to say this straight: I've got my own shotgun. If something like THAT comes onto my property, it ain't leavin.'"

Susan had been expecting this.

"I'd like to point out that that would be illegal."

"And Ma'am? I'd like to point out I've got my own backhoe as well. Good luck finding what happened to them."

Mutterings of agreements began to swell.

Susan sighed.

She said, "I'd also add that these will benefit the land in a large variety of ways. They will naturally deposit manure randomly in the scrublands. They tend to roam a great deal. And will spread across a large part of the land, acting like Johnny Appleseed spreading grasses, trees and vegetation as they wander. These are gentle creatures and not a particular threat to your livestock."

Walter spoke again.

"And Ma'am, I'd also add they will ignore electric fences, and push through anything not set in cement and re-bar, eat a raspberry bush like the thorns don't exist, and have skin thicker than a Rhino!"

At that, the crowd turned and looked at him. Walter pulled

out his smartphone.

"Wikipedia! I looked the damn things up during the slide-show," he said.

The crowd turned back to face Susan.

Susan continued, "They will thrive in the deserts around here turning them into gardens wherever they roam, as long as they can roam a bit. They could travel a hundred miles over the course of a month. Part of the deal I'm asking from you is to let them. Their feet will ignore cattle guards, those metal poles over a pit that a cow won't walk on, so they will tend to wander in and out of your pastures without needing you to do anything. Adding more of those cattle guards instead of fencing, might be more effective in the long run. You already tag more of your cows with a GPS ear clip, so they won't wander far off your property."

Someone else yelled up from the audience.

"Ma'am that ain't helping your case, that's still gonna be dozens of fences these meat tanks plough through. What happens when they decide somebody's flower garden tastes better than these grasses and weeds you hope they will eat instead? Not much chance to shoo off something three times as heavy as a bear and covered in armor, if it decided to eat your cabbages!"

"They tend to be slow, but they do travel long distances and they avoid obstacles. They won't be pushing down too many fences. Only the ones they don't notice. Barbed wire and electric fences mainly."

At that the muttering grew louder.

Another voice from the crowd replied, "Ma'am, three quarters of the fences in Texas are barbed wire or electric."

"True. But you do realize that's why desertification has increased, right? The restriction of herd animals is causing natural grasslands to erode at terrifying rates. We have to have a return to roaming. Buffalo, cattle, and, yes, Glyptodonts must be allowed to graze in the scrub, either by moving them directly from field to field which helps, but does not cover enough unclaimed land. Or, by reintroducing something that doesn't care. Ignoring fencing is not a bug, it's a feature."

Another rancher stood up, half the people in the audience were standing now. He had to speak loudly over the muttering.

"No Ma'am, anything that busts our fences without noticing ain't gonna be welcome on our property," he said emphatically

She sighed. "Let me put this another way. They reach maturity in four years and need to raise their young for the entire time. They show signs they can age to thirty or so, we aren't sure. They breed in litters of four to six, so they grow relatively fast for such a large land animal."

Someone else responded.

"So these things will triple in number every four years, and you think that's a good thing?"

Several people rumbled in agreement.

Susan had to speak up, even with the microphone on, "They can likely be bred to mature faster, but we don't see a point. Although you might."

"What the hell do you mean by that?" Walter said.

Susan continued, "They are docile and domesticate easily. We can turn them away from those 'cabbages' with a garden hose or a loud noise. A guy with a broom in a Glyptodont's face will easily chase them away. They can share a field with cows just fine and prefer to eat the things the cows don't like. The hides are very tough and durable, similar to alligator or rhino with interesting and marketable patterns and colors. The bone is dense and would work well as a replacement for ivory.

They thrive in wasteland scrub and turn it back to prairie and forest land over time. There is no apex predator right now that can take one down. You don't have to feed them and they find their own water just fine."

She paused before she said her last bit, her ace in the hole. "They taste fantastic." Susan spoke up to call her assistant.

"David?"

Everything got quiet as David emerged from the front door with a large picnic cooler. Stopping at every row to hand out tiny hoagie rolls with some sort of brisket on it. The smell permeated the hall instantly. Mouth watering.

It was ten minutes before anyone spoke as everyone ate their little sandwiches. There was no dissent. They tasted delicious.

Walter spoke first.

"Why didn't you say so in the first place? How much for a breeding pair?"

Discussion broke out all over the hall. What kind of fences could keep cows in but let the damn things wander in and out?

They were discussing the feasibility of swapping the bottom

of electric fence posts with a metal spring as Susan smiled and left Grange Hall.

One down, sixty more to visit, before the reintroduction began. This went a lot easier than she had anticipated. In fifty or so years, there should be enough Glyptodonts in the wild to start actually becoming a problem. But this should make a huge difference in turning the land from desert back into a very pleasant place.

They could worry about that fifty years from now, when people will see these giant armadillo's as a regular thing, spotting them from the highway the way we do cows now. She smiled to herself.

When they become a pest, well, that will be her next phase. She needs the Glyptodonts. Needs them badly. So she can reintroduce her real target.

Sabertooth tigers.

☞

Coming Out

John knocked, and waited.

He knew something was up. Charly had made the net call pretty late at night. A little hesitant, asking him to come over. He had been expecting something like this for weeks. He'd seen the signs. He knew what Charly wanted and he knew he could help. If John was wrong though, well, tonight would turn out awkward.

He had called for an autocab before Charly had even finished the call, using gesture controls so as not to interrupt. He'd cleared his calendar at the same time, and tapped the air to have his voicemail call up Steve and cancel his previous plans. If he was right, Steve was going to be ecstatic! The auto-cab was waiting for him by the time he stepped out his front door. He had put on a masking screen before he got in the cab, preventing any and all cameras or sensors from getting a good look at him, a common thing, nowadays, ever since the privacy war. Well not a war exactly, more like the privacy flashmob and sit-in.

The autocab ride didn't take long, and there he was. Less than ten minutes after the call. On Charly's doorstep.

John felt like he'd been waiting forever. The door finally opened. Charly stood on the other side, a little embarrassed. He gave John a little hopeful smile, and let him in. John took a deep breath, and entered, popping his mask as he stepped inside.

John sat on one end of the couch, a dominant piece of fur-niture. He was a little amused that the couch faced a screen, a big one. He noticed speakers in the corners of the room, at least six.

"That's cool," John said. "A flat screen TV with surround sound."

Charly tossed him a beer. John caught it easily.

"Yeah. I know. Old tech. An antique. I like sitting here and watching, uh, stuff." Charly hesitated. John wanted to tell him he knew already. But it was important that Charly say it. "I'm a—."

Charly started to say it, that three letter word so full of meaning, but he chickened out.

"—I'm an antique lover. The glasses don't capture the same effect. Not really. And the contacts are worse. Glad you know what it is."

John chose not to press him.

"No, no. I've always liked how important this was in the Twentieth and Twenty-First Centuries. It's, uh, good to remember."

Charly sat on the same couch, other end, and tapped the top of his beer can. A small actuator slid aside and allowed vents to let compressed air release quickly. Once freed from the coiled tube inside, the sudden pressure release caused the can to cool quickly. In a few seconds it was frosty. The can changed colors, letting Charly know the beer was ready to drink. Later, when he was finished with it, that same actuator would reverse, squeezing all air out and causing the titanium can to compress down to the size of a pea, ready for recycling.

John popped his can too.

Charly took a deep breath and looked at John.

"I need to tell you something—"

John focused. This was it.

"Sure Charly. What's up?"

"I'm a fan."

Calmly John looked Charly in the eye. He didn't want to scare him. He had said it, things would be OK.

"I suspected you were."

"You knew?" Charly looked surprised. "I thought I had it pretty well hidden. The people at work, they don't understand."

"You'd be surprised at what some of those same people are into."

"I see you all the time. And I figured if anyone was, it would be you. Once, I could tell you were wearing a jersey, under your shirt."

John smiled. He remembered that day, he'd made sure Charly saw it, and changed right after to keep anyone else from knowing.

"So, what kind of fan?"

"Football, mostly. A little hockey. Baseball. Basketball."

"You know why they were made illegal?" Charly asked.

"Yeah. I know. Repetitive head injuries. Displays of naked aggression. Broken bones. Riots after games. Competition is seen as the root of selfish behavior. Blah. Blah. Blah. It was made illegal a long time ago. For the children."

"And things changed," John stated. "People began to look at fans like there was something wrong with them."

"There's nothing wrong with me!" Charly glared.

"Easy, easy," John spoke calmly. "I know. Trust me. I know. But after the crackdown on the networks and the changes in laws. All the court cases, and then the aversion therapy. It's been pretty hard on fans. They say now that they can 'cure' it. They say aggressive competition is a gateway to criminal behavior."

"No. I don't want to be cured. I've been keeping it pretty secret for so long. Found some darknet sites. They put entire seasons up on multiple streaming casts. Encrypted and well hidden. They get taken down once in a while, but I find them again."

"Sports Central?" John smiled.

"Yeah!" Charly smiled back. "And ESPN archives."

"Really!" John smiled. "I'd lost track of that after the last crackdown. I'm gonna need the address for that."

"No problem."

"So, um. How big a fan are you?"

"Nothing too crazy," Charly hastened to add. "I got some memorabilia stashed away, a baseball signed, a couple a jerseys, a keychain with a few thousand games on it. Stuff I can hide easy."

"Yeah, good plan. If you get caught with it, next thing you know they think you are bringing kids home and making them watch it with you."

"I know. I know. I won't go that far." Charly hesitated before asking, "Um, how far have you gone?"

John looked Charly straight in the eye, "I've played."

"No way! How did you get enough people together for teams?"

"I know a few guys. There are a lot of us. Lot of women too. We meet in secret and have resorts we go to. Weekend excursions where it's just us, some benches and a field. No webcams or e-glasses allowed. EMP field for blocking signals. A mask covering the whole area. Not just teams. Leagues."

"Holy crap. That explains the bruises that time—"

"—Yup. Told people I fell down the stairs, and I'm allergic to the repair nano. But it was really football."

"Wow. Football. You, uh, you wanna watch a game?"

"We soundproof here? I tend to yell."

"Hell, yeah!"

"Awesome. Start it up. Say, can I call Steve to come over?"

"Steve? Steve's a fan?

"The biggest. He'll bring pretzels."

"Hot damn, call him up!"

"How about Susan?"

"She's kind of flaming, wears her jersey in public and all. Will she be, y'know, discreet?"

"Not a problem."

"Okay, but we gotta keep this secret."

"You got it. We'll just tell people it's an orgy."

"Okay. Good. I'll make popcorn."

☞

Watch This

There he is.

Eric spotted him at the gate. Jack Lyttle. Here for the big game. The bastard was smiling as he handed over his ticket. He probably thought he was going to be enjoying this day. Eric had other plans for Jack.

He knew Jack had a season ticket. Six months after the last time Eric had gone to a game he had seen Jack there, oblivious to him, a dozen rows down, along with several of his buddies. Laughing and drinking.

Eric seethed at that memory. He'd be in pain for the rest of his life because of Jack. He'd never be able to walk without a limp. Dentures replaced all his broken teeth. Loss of vision in one eye. A bland, soft food diet. A colostomy bag. All because of Jack and his laughing friends.

He had lawsuits against Officer Jack. Improper procedure, illegal entry, police brutality. He had been hopeful about the lawsuits. He really had. But one of the people Jack was drinking with was the very judge who had denied each of his cases.

Eric had been in the wrong place at the wrong time. He'd been walking home at night, a techie who kept odd hours. Officer Jack drove by, stopped his patrol car, and demanded to know what he was doing. Eric told Jack he was doing nothing wrong, and to go to hell. That was the first beating.

The second one was in his home. Eric had filed a lawsuit. Somehow Jack found out the same day he filed. Jack had broken down the front door and beaten him again, far more brutally. Laughing and yelling the whole time, "There ain't nuthin' you can do!"

Even with Eric's home cameras recording every blow, the judge had dismissed the case. That judge. The one drinking beer and slapping Jack on the back in the stadium.

Jack had gone federal at that point, an agent of the FBI had contacted him. Eric was told that due to the uncooperative police department, it would take years before his case would ever reach a trial. He researched Jack Lyttle then, hoping to prepare a massive case, this time his plan was to show it to the local newspaper. Maybe they could bring him some justice. That was the third beating. Someone at the newspaper had warned Jack.

After he'd recovered, Eric had tried to do something normal again. He'd gone to a game to clear his mind, to watch the teams play. He sat there wondering what other options he had, beginning to despair, when he had first spotted Jack.

Till the end of the game, Eric had pulled up his hood and gone quiet, staring at Jack's back. He knew from what he saw then, there would be no legal justice for him. No day in court. His research had brought up other cases against Officer Lyttle. And two other lawsuits had been dropped. Both for "lack of evidence" even though there was camera footage. And both of the accusers could no longer be found. Either they were hiding from Jack, or Jack had killed them. Jack had hinted at that, telling Eric he would not walk away if there needed to be a fourth visit.

And Eric watched Jack laughing and joking with the people Eric had hoped would help him. Both the judge, and the federal agent. All three side by side, laughing and enjoying the game. Eric realized the FBI agent may be nothing of the sort, maybe just a friend of Jack's, pretending to help Eric, while telling Jack his every move. He realized, in any case, he would get no help from him.

That's when he decided on a different path.

He prepared for some time. It was a modern arena, full of cameras and technology. But the sysadmin hadn't fully locked down the network. Eric gained access to a wiring closet easily enough. Full of equipment. Routers. Switches. A couple terminals. A server rack. Eric had always been a master of these. He had pulled out his smartphone and taken pics of every label he could find. Mac addresses, model numbers, wireless keys and passwords.

Someone had left a clipboard hanging from a nail with the names and ID's of every tech with access to the closet. It was supposed to be for security, a log of who came in, when they left. Wow, that was a score. And, sure enough, Eric found a piece of paper taped underneath a keyboard with numbers and letters. Another score. Sloppy password protection. Eric smiled at that. "Hard to guess. Changes often. Not written down. Choose any two." He shook his head. He had access to half the network that very night.

Working steadily, he had managed to gain one login after another. It took only a few days before he could remote into every camera, every server, every piece of equipment in the stadium. The scoreboard. The plasmatron. The spotlights. He had control of it all.

He kept up the pretense of the appeals. Meeting with the judge, meeting with the 'federal agent,' recording everything. Every lie. Every betrayal. They would tell him they were working on his case, and yet, every game, there were the judge and the agent, sitting side by side with Jack.

Now. Today. At the bottom of the plasmatron, he inserted a short message that scrolled every few minutes. "For free wifi connection, log into Arena-Network." Jack didn't have a smartphone, as far as Eric could tell. Jack wouldn't care about the scrolling message. Well, not at first. He had prepared anyway, a tight deadzone prevented anyone in the seats around Jack from getting online. A small box under Jack's seat the size of a deck of cards made it difficult to connect to any wireless signal for at least a five foot radius.

Weeks ago, Eric had installed dozens of routers onto the network, breaking in late at night. It was easy when he already controlled the electronic locks.

He'd made his own badge, buying a batch of cards online and matching those serial numbers up to the security program. He simply changed the serial number of the card to match an arena employee, and changed it back when he was done. Had there been a guard, he might have noticed that his badge was a plain white card. But the arena was modern, and they trusted the technology.

He'd hooked his wifi up to the arena network and made sure it all worked. The only differences were, in the rest of the arena, the hotspots were completely open. Anyone could use them. But of course now they routed through his own gateway before they connected to the internet supplied by the arena. An amazing connection, that. The latest in technology. Eric was impressed.

When he was done, his routers were running far more efficiently and giving a better connection than even the original format. He smiled. In his profession, he always tried to leave things better than before he had touched them. Amazing the kind of motivation he had now. The software he installed that improved the cameras almost felt like an act of love. The control center was going to get a gift. He wondered if they would appreciate it. He hoped so.

As he set his plan in motion, it crossed his mind that he might not be allowed to live to the end of the week. He didn't much care.

First quarter of the game.

An app on his smartphone allowed Eric to see a few hundred people were using his free connection. Not enough. He changed the plasmatron scroll to be continuous. "Free Wifi. Connect to Arena-Network to watch any camera in the stadium." He then added the first splash-page. That page had little thumbnails which allowed people to watch the live feed from any of the two hundred cameras in and around the stadium. Ten thousand people began to play, bringing up and watching one after another of the raw feeds. He could see them nudging one another and getting a huge kick out of showing their friends one particular angle or another.

Eric nodded to himself. It was working.

Before halftime, thirty thousand people were huddled around one handheld device or another, laughing as they chose their own views and camera angles. He could see people grinning as they used the little tool-sets Eric had provided to digitally pan and zoom the cameras, or reverse and slow motion a particular image. He couldn't help smiling to himself. Now only a few of the cameras were pointed at the game. Most were focused on the fans. Thousands of people in real time remixing the game and acting as their own control studio.

During halftime, Eric started his own endgame.

A new splash-page appeared on every single device. "Before continuing, please watch this five minute video. Arena-Network promises you will remember this for a long time." Nothing else would work on their devices until people clicked on the video. Fast forwarding was disabled. The cheerleaders doing their halftime thing were, for the most part, ignored.

"Hello. My name is Eric. I can no longer see out of my right eye. I can no longer stand straight. Jack Lyttle is responsible." That was how the clip started. The video was a masterpiece of editing. Step by step it explained what happened. Clips from the video showing the first beating, the second, the third. The lawsuits. The betrayals. The hospital stay. The bruises. The doctors explaining how much his life had to change.

While the video ran, documents appeared one after the other below the stream. They showed Jack's record of brutality as a cop, the many complaints against him, transcripts, court records. A masterwork of video design. The entire stadium began to grow quiet as the clip played from so many devices simultaneously.

Jack and his friends never noticed. They were drinking and laughing, looking at the girls doing back flips, not paying attention to the crowd. Three minutes into the video, just as the teams were coming back onto the field, the lights dimmed except for a single spotlight focused on Jack Lyttle.

Jack watched his face on the Plasmatron. He looked up and then aped a silly look to the camera, then flexed his muscles and enjoyed himself. He nudged his friends. They laughed too, but nobody else in the stadium did. It was surprisingly quiet but Jack and his pals did not notice. Eric put the remainder of the beating video in a window below Jack's live face.

Jack still was not aware of what was happening.

The crowd watched, silent and angry as slowly Jack noticed the other video. A split screen of his own face, live on the Plasmatron, above the tape of him beating the hell out of Eric, lying on the ground in the clip. They watched Jack grow horrified in real time, proving to fifty thousand people that the video was the truth.

The tape below Jack's real-time face of horror, showed Jack laughing as he kicked Eric, over and over again. The live screen showed Jack aghast. The tape showed images of the judge and the agent sharing beers, recorded from game after game. Splice. Jack laughing. Splice. Eric bloody and in a hospital. Splice. Jack drinking a beer with the judge. Splice. The judge denying Eric's appeal. Splice. Jack drinking and laughing with the agent. Splice. The agent saying to Eric that there was nothing he could do. And after each five second vignette, spliced with different footages of a kick to Eric's ribs. All the while the live split showing Jack, and now his buddies, panic stricken.

"There ain't nuthin' you can do!" repeated from the loud-speakers continuously at the end, along with the sound of the pounding of a courtroom gavel. Jack's sadistic taunt grew louder each time.

Twelve seconds were left on the video when the first bottle hit him. Jack tried to run. He didn't make it to the stairs. Neither did the agent. The judge made it a little farther.

☞

Mapping People

David sat beside Susan. People mapping.

They loved people mapping. It helped pass the time. Susan was smiling in her special way, following David's line of sight. As soon as Susan spotted the same girl David was looking at, Susan reported with a grin. "She's got her clothing set for Modest."

David whispered back, "Put her in a bustle."

Susan giggled and her hands chopped the air, accessing the controls on the app she was sharing with David. She accessed the correct files. And, instantly, the woman across the mall had her clothing transformed from a simple pantsuit to a proper

19th century outfit, complete with a parasol and straw hat. As the lady moved about, it was comical to watch the parasol try to maintain its correct position in her hand. The bustle bounced around with a rhythm all its own.

David was finding her new attire appealing. "This outfit was in the Modest file?"

Susan grinned. "Sure was! Midwest Pre-Megafauna Cowboy Collection, from Ayar Done Right.

As the suddenly school-marmed woman stopped and adjusted her own Ayar controls, it looked to the world as though she was battling an invisible opponent with the bumbershoot umbrella. She had realized she'd been tagged through a signal alert in her glasses and so she had called up a virtual mirror. As with David and Susan's, her augmented reality glasses seamlessly merged networks with the thousands of cameras in the mall, to bitmap her image along with the shared virtual outfit that Susan had put her in. All of this displayed, of course, only on the insides of their own glasses.

The lady nodded, looking at herself and how she was mapped, it was clear she was amused and decided to keep Susan's selection. She held her hand so that the parasol twirled over one shoulder and as she walked off she smiled in their direction.

A fun one!

David had been doing this with Susan for a good twenty minutes now. Not to everyone, of course. Some people set their profiles to No and Susan and David couldn't play with their clothing or image at all. Some had specific Ayar designs, things they had paid for that, once set, could only be manipulated in predefined ways. But sometimes, sometimes people had their profiles turned all the way down to Anything Goes.

What David liked best were the people who weren't wearing Ayar glasses and had no idea they were being mapped. But those were so rare now that he hadn't seen any in months.

Susan let David dress her any way he wanted. She'd dance and spin in whatever he picked for her, showing off the mapped outfit no matter how revealing or risqué it was.

In the time they'd been there they had changed people into clowns, powdered-wig judges, dapper secret agents, stone Greek gods, Egyptian mummies, and, for David's amusement, a massive number of sexy suits. So far today, Susan's was the only map set low enough to model those.

David sighed, Susan was the only one he had seen today who was set to Anything Goes. He had seen a girl last week who had been set that low. She probably had forgotten to update her profile after a party.

He had put the party girl in a cat suit, complete with anamorphic tail, silk teddy and amazing cleavage. She had seen him watching her, however, and, after checking her glasses, was not amused. She had made quite a spectacle of jabbing the air as she selected from the menus in her own Ayar controls, then glared at David before leaving in a bit of a huff.

After the girl left, Susan began laughing so hard she fell to the ground and literally rolled around. When he checked his own profile's history, he saw that the cat girl had not only set her own profile to a full No but had put him in a flasher's overcoat, complete with oversized binoculars and no pants. The Ayar had deliberate pixelation hiding what would have been his privates–and the program was not kind with the size. David was not amused.

Susan bought a whole bunch of Ayar outfits. Twenty creds apiece. David paid for them all. He had given her a budget of ten bucks which was ten sets at a hundred creds apiece. Susan had found and purchased dozens of virtual outfits on sale, giving them away to any passing shopper who would take one.

The outfits each had an encryption tag. They would only map themselves on to one image. If you wanted to put the

Ayar map on someone else, you'd have to pay for it again. Or hack it. And for 20 creds? It wasn't worth the time.

On the other hand, once you had applied it, it became a part of your profile. Those who were mapped could use them as much as they wanted, and anyone whose glasses could see your profile, would see whatever it had as its current map.

David did this all the time with Susan. It was their "thing." It was harmless and fun. Ayar cost almost nothing. Ten bucks could barely buy a meal from a food dispenser! Besides, who could say no to Susan?

"Want me to change my dress again?"

"Sure," said David.

"The creds you gave me are all used up," Susan said.

"OK, then, tell you what, let's just model a few of them on five-second-bursts and I'll only buy the ones I really like."

Susan smiled and clapped her hands five or six times and made the adjustments.

For just a few seconds she was wearing a tight white jump-suit, made of something like nylon. David thought her baseline outfit had some appeal all by itself, but then it started cycling through all the things she had picked out from the demo stream.

"Let's do red," she said with a conspiratorial wink. Suddenly her dress was bathed in virtual flames, licking her body all over, then a pair of virtual horns and a thin tail that ended in a metal arrow head completed the look. The flames teased and danced around her curves. The tail snapped like a whip. Susan looked him straight in the eye and pretended she was about to pounce on him. David didn't particularly like it when she did that.

Besides, he'd seen that sort of outfit many times, devil maps were last week's fashion. Susan already had a dozen variations.

"No, it's, like, too devil. Go with music. Or maybe . . . nature?"

"How about blue?" Susan spun around, her virtual dress flaring out around her, the color changing from a deep crimson to a powder blue before she had finished her twirl. Tiny shapes danced around the bottom of the dress, forming cartoonish musical notes that swelled into soap bubbles and popped in pure musical tones, just barely above conscious notice. It was a very pretty effect, although David found it distracting.

"It's fine," David said. Susan really looked as though she was enjoying all this and she had such a flair for this sort of thing.

"Maybe green, then, for nature?" Susan tapped out a command in the air around her, calling up another design. Her dress changed, in a top-down wipe, into a forest canopy of leaves, swaying in a non-existent wind. It also mapped her hair a bright green. Caressing her all over, small and clustered leaves at her waist and hips, larger with more space around her chest, showing just enough skin to make David crane a little with each simulated flutter. David caught himself. The illusion had gotten to him. Even though he knew the leaves weren't real, he had felt his heart race a bit when he thought they would fall off or blow away.

"I vote for Nature!"

Susan looked up, her own glasses had screens on both the inside and outside, and so her eyes were enhanced a bit, slightly larger in the display than they really were. That was the style these days, almost everyone did the "Manga Look," the big eyes, small mouth. It gave her a sheen of innocence that had gotten David's attention in the first place.

"So you vote for this one?" she smiled in that flirty way she always used just before she asked him to buy her something.

David sighed. "How much is it?"

Susan held her hand in front of her. David knew she was projecting the catalog information onto the inside of her wrist. "It's a hundred creds, because it has several sub-menus with a lot of extra features. It's not a oneshot." She looked up through her eyelashes at him.

"Oh, all right."

David slashed his fingers through the air in his command gesture and tapped a couple of icons that appeared. His account was accessed and the item he framed between his thumb and forefinger was selected. And now? Nature was his. As long as Susan didn't block him, he could put her in that dress any time he wanted. He was thinking about the cat-girl who had been so mad, and wondered if she would have been less annoyed at him if he had put her in this number.

The virtual leaves of Susan's dress shivered in delightful ways.

"I'm not buying any more dresses today," said David. "Let's walk to the Ayar environment store."

Susan gave a little pout, her hands held behind her back, the better to show off the bare spaces between the leaves.

The store was nearby. David stumbled a little as he was entering the shop and his glasses slipped a bit. For just a brief second he saw the place as it really was, white geometric shapes on top of white rubber pads, a little stained and dirty since it had apparently not been cleaned in a while. David quickly pushed his glasses back up, fumbling a little in his haste. When they were back in place, he noticed that Susan had come close, just a few inches away with her hands on her knees.

She asked him, "Are you OK?"

David had trouble paying attention to anything but her cleavage for a second. She saw where he was looking and gave him a slow smile. David began to smile back, then quickly turned to the display that was materializing in front of him.

And the longer he looked, he saw a forest glade, with trees that went up for miles, single shafts of light poking through the canopy, a willow tree in the center of a tiny island, which in turn was in a slightly larger crystal-clear pond with mossy banks. Rabbits, butterflies, and unicorns seemed to be really wandering around the scene. It was delightful.

David had not seen that particular design from the store before. He liked it a lot. Idly he gestured and pinched the air and a menu of options appeared, Captain Nemo's Study, Dr.

Seuss, Tarzan's Jungle, Retro Utopia —Ah, here was its name, Enchanted Grove!

"Which one are you looking at, David?" asked Susan. "I'm looking at Wonderland myself."

David had forgotten they might be looking at two different worlds.

"Oh, Wonderland's nice," replied David absentmindedly as he continued to fiddle with the settings, "But this Enchanted Grove is great with your new—"

—He interrupted himself, "Wow, the menu has a dragon!" David jabbed the air with his finger.

Susan had already dialed up the same overlay as well, and gave a little gasp as a fifty-foot dragon pushed aside a couple of the large trees to crane its neck at them. And was the dragon smiling?

David decided he didn't care for the dragon, "Meh," he said, and, with a flick, it was gone.

"You should get this!" Susan squealed, spinning in circles as she gestured at the entire scene. "It would look so great mapping your living room!"

"Naw," answered David, still absorbed in the forest primeval and not really listening to Susan. "A full map skin is spendy, and I bought Captain Nemo's Study already. I'm still loving the way all the fish in the window look, and how the water makes patterns on all my stuff."

"Oh," said Susan, looking a little disappointed. She started on something else, "Want to get a new game?"

"Actually, I'm going to go home. I have to get up early in the morning."

"Are you sure? We haven't gone into the entertainment store in a while. I heard some of your favorite movie productions have new endings!" At the end of the sentence her voice had gone all sing-song and her still vibrant leaves were shimmying.

"No. But thanks."

The leaves shook a little more as though the wind were picking up. "We could go into the printshop? There's a new exercise exoskeleton that uses isometric haptics for resistance training. They have one printed out already that could fit you. We could try it out. It would help you lose some weight."

"No. I've spent enough money today, Susan. I might come back in a day or two."

"Oh, all right. I'll be waiting for you," she said, and blew him a kiss that had the effect of a leaf blowing at him with dewdrops on it.

David sighed as he walked away from Susan, knowing that if he turned around she would still be there. She'd be waiting for him. Waiting in that exact spot even if he didn't come back for a year. Just like she'd be waiting for him at whatever store he went to.

He liked Susan, he really did. But sometimes the sex kitten stuff was a little too strong. Maybe he should change his sales avatar to something else for a while? Maybe the English Butler or the Heavyset Grandmother?

But who was he kidding? He wouldn't do that. He knew he'd never abandon Susan. Not until he met a real girl.

☞

Open Road

The car pulled into the gas station. On Board Systems wirelessly connected its owner's account to the convenience store. Transaction was approved, the pump autonomously lined its robot arm out to the pattern around the gas cap.

The cap irised open, the nozzle was inserted. Syngas permeated the fuel cells. The artificial hydrocarbons didn't take long. A few minutes later the tank was finished. It would be three months before it needed to do that again.

No one paid much attention to the car. It was popular a while back, one of the first models of its type. A not particularly flashy shade of blue, coated with a layer of clear hydrophobic polymers. It never got dirty. The motors were ceramic, copper and molybdenum. One motor for each wheel. The frame was a titanium alloy. The panels were a resin made of spider silk and carbon fiber, so were the tires, but in a different mix. The windows were aluminum oxide, transparent sheets far stronger than steel.

This model still had a full steering wheel and a driver's seat, an oddity nowadays; in fact, one of the last models that did that. But few would know because no one could see inside. The privacy settings had the windows set to full mirror mode.

Had anyone noticed this car among all the others, they would probably not have realized it had pulled into the same gas station three months before, and three months before that. Had a traffic analysis program taken a good look, it would have spotted that this car was looping the highways. North on 405, South on I5. Pulling off only to refill.

The car showed no sign of wear. It probably wouldn't for a hundred years.

The driver had known exactly what he was doing. The pattern he had programmed took several hours to complete. His account held plenty of money to keep the fuel going for some time.

He was in the driver's seat, in what looked like quiet

contemplation. He loved his car, he loved to drive. Well he loved to ride nowadays. He could think of no better way than this. Laid off. Another job lost to the robots. He had at first spent a lot of time just going around the loop, wondering what to do.

He hoped no one would notice for a couple of years. If he was lucky, he and his car might make it ten.

When he had drunk the tea he had prepared there was no pain, and he had kept his eyes on the road and wide open.

☞

The Doll

Hattie worked on the doll.

She had everything she needed. She had pulled the hairs from his hairbrush when he let her use his bathroom and had found a piece of toilet paper with a red spot of blood on it, probably from shaving. She smiled at that, it made this so much easier to have some blood.

He was leaving her. She knew that he had met someone else but wasn't sure who yet. She'd make a doll for her too, later. It wasn't nice to play with her affections. This was payback time.

Hattie came from a family with a tradition of knowing what to do about these things, knowledge passed down mother to daughter, aunt to niece, for hundreds of years. Midwives. Wise women. She had a network, and they came through for her. Her sisters were legion.

She hummed to herself as she opened up his doll. Peeling off and setting aside the false outer skin to reveal the real doll underneath. She had scanned a photo of him into her computer and his face was now printed directly onto the vinyl skin which now sagged in a wad. Sad. And helpless. She smiled while she looked at it. And then pushed his head in with one finger, hard, until his face couldn't be seen anymore.

Nobody left her. Nobody.

She tapped his doll and said in a whisper, "Hocus pocus!"

It began to glow.

These dolls were a marvel. Secret of course. No talk about them online. No images. No written directions anywhere. No doll was mailed. Hand delivered every time. Sisters only. Made with ritual and rite. The old ways were best.

His blood had been extracted into a special saline solution where it was coaxed into growing again until she had the right amount. Just a drop or two was all she needed, but she had ten times that now just to be sure.

She dribbled two drops onto the doll's chest, splatting into the microchannel grooves that she had prepared. Capillary action sucked it into patterns and deposited it into a the complex framework. Little lines radiated from the splatter into dozens of tiny chambers, scattered across the surface of the doll's arms and legs and head. Chakra points. Acupuncture spots. Each treated with a reactor and a sensor. The lines followed old patterns taken from ancient rituals.

She continued to hum as she opened the head to feed his hair sample into the doll. Once the head was closed back up, all the air was evacuated, then the contents remaining were flashburned by a laser in a tiny chamber, the resulting gas then deposited onto a prepared surface, and spectroscopically analyzed. A lot can be learned from a hair.

The microchannels in the doll had moved the blood to the various stations, chemical analysis began on all points.

The sisters had been working on the systems in these dolls for some time. They had evolved a bit over the years. One must keep up with the times. And the sisters had been doing this for centuries. They were proud that they were always were just a bit ahead of the curve.

She tapped her computer display and began to read the

analysis. She knew quite a bit about his diet already, but his mild diabetes was a surprise. That might be handy.

The DNA records were compared to other databases she had uploaded into the doll already. EEG records had been delivered by sisters who worked in hospitals who always kept a spare before uploading to the "Private" folders. Details on the electrical activity and patterns of his neural network were a piece of cake.

She had hidden a sensor on his bed. A sensitive thing measuring his heart beat, breathing patterns, and even his subvocals while he dreamed. Hattie also had hidden a camera watching from a second sensor she had stuck to the ceiling fan originally not intended for this purpose. She sighed, oh so briefly, then got back to it. But the camera was one that also mapped and monitored his thermal patterns while he slept, among other, well, things.

She had his DNA now. Haplogroups were well mapped and checked against a vast database to determine precisely what he was likely to respond to. The chemical traces in the hair sample added even more information like what he had responded to in the past, sometimes it could tell what he had liked as a kid.

Subsonics and radio frequencies generated by the doll could

resonate exactly to his own specific patterns. Tailor made chemicals could be released. Even viruses could be created to react with him alone.

Having the doll in the same room as him for a few minutes was all she'd need. To start.

The doll already could allow for sudden temporary effects, it was able to remotely disrupt the nervous system in his arms, legs, and head, causing pain in the spots on the doll she would touch with the stylus. Well, for a couple seconds anyway, then his body would compensate.

His neural map was tuned as well. She could induce a strong pheromone response when he was close to the doll. Fear. Lust. Anger. Confusion. All with a button press. The sisters had dealing with this kind of thing down.

Except love was harder. She'd have to work at that, day by day, using the doll slowly over time. Fine tuning the effects, and mapping and analyzing the feedback. Love was more of an art than a skill. She had to be careful not to overplay her hand. She'd *make* him love her, and leave that other one wondering what the hell had happened. She'd make him her boy toy. And when she was done? She'd use the doll one last time.

She could make every one of his dreams, a dream of her. A

wash of endorphins whenever he whispered her name.

Her computer dinged. The doll had a report ready.

As it continued its analysis programs, she poured herself a glass of Chardonnay and read through the record. A heart murmur. Well, now she had the final button to program for her doll.

It wasn't nice to play with someone's emotions, Hattie thought. She took a long sip of her wine, thought about all the pleasure she was going to have with him, then smiled long and slow and cold at the doll. He shouldn't be playing games, not when he was so far, so very far, out of his league.

☞

Third Time's the Charm

They had been watching for a long time, debating on whether or not to do it. Factions argued and debated, pondering the flaws compared to the merits. Every point carefully sifted and measured. The reasons were many, as were the reasons not to. This was taken seriously.

At the destruction of Hiroshima and Nagasaki, the process sped up. The luxury of millennia was over. A decision was imminent.

Less than a hundred years passed before judgment was rendered.

In sixty places a small cylinder was dropped into the sky, places where the wind was strong. The cylinders sublimated quickly, dissolving into what appeared to be nothingness.

Not exactly nothingness.

Just particles smaller than the eye could see. Particles that multiplied, again and again. Tiny constructs that launched themselves into the wind, dived into water, and burrowed into the earth. It took all those years to make a decision that was irrevocable in two days.

At the stroke of the forty-eighth hour, the particles could be found within any cubic inch of soil on earth, in the deepest ocean trenches, and at the top of the highest mountains. No island was spared, no mine-shaft, no secret hidden place. Anywhere on earth, everywhere on earth, the constructs could be found. If anyone had known to look.

At the stroke of the seventy-second hour, the constructs did their job, and crumbled. They dissolved into polymers that warped into compounds that melted into individual carbon atoms and a few trace elements, and vanished without a hint of their origin or purpose.

It took three months before anybody noticed something was different.

Hospitals weren't as busy as they should be. Most of the usual things continued. People were still treated for cancer, for drug overdoses, for prostate troubles, obesity and face lifts, but something was missing.

Two more months went by before the hospitals knew for sure, and they were the first to realize.

Children.

They were still being born, at seemingly normal rates, nothing exciting or unusual. And yet, no one was coming in for the first time. Nobody who panicked and ran for a blood test because their protection failed. No one went berserk because their test came back with a positive result. No newlyweds who were trying were successful. No matter how many fertility shots were administered, they just wouldn't take. Strange. But there was no way to evaluate it. It wasn't medical. It wasn't science. The hospitals kept quiet about it.

No viruses were discovered, no chemical imbalances were detected. Hormones were normal, menstruation was fine, sperm counts were average, but nowhere was there a first-trimester pregnancy. Two more months went by before the story broke outside the hospital rope line.

No one believed the headlines at first. *Why that's silly!* they would say, silently demanding that their voices not crack at the mere thought it might be true. Just last week that young lady in apartment 4a had a healthy baby girl. They simply regarded this as another attempt to sell news through scare tactics.

On April 14th, at 7:53 AM, after a simple delivery, David Pinkham was born at the Sacred Heart Hospital in Shreveport, Illinois. A healthy six-pound four-ounce baby boy.

He was the last child born on earth.

At first people joked about it. Today is nobody's birthday. No buns in the oven. Things like that. But the jokes didn't last long. Scientists began to look for the cause in earnest. Every nation had their best people on the job. No research was hidden, all cooperated. Sperm banks were set up everywhere, in the hopes that one man or woman was spared, or that a particular combination would work. Vast and detailed information on human reproduction was gathered, stymied only by the inability to watch it in action. All that international effort, but not even zygotes would form.

Nothing.

Well, they found part of the problem: people had been altered genetically. Something basic had been changed. What that something was? The scientists didn't know and could not figure out. How it happened? They had no clue. How to fix it? Well, they did not shout this from the rooftops, but they said it among themselves that this was beyond them. Nothing they knew helped. No pattern, no medical advance, nada.

Animals were not affected. As far as man could tell, the wild creatures were spared. Insane, desperate attempts to merge animal and human DNA were completely unsuccessful.

David Pinkham was kidnapped when he was two years old. A young woman was apprehended, frantic, wild-eyed, and tearful. "It's not fair!" she screamed over and over. "Why do they have one and I can't!" David was returned to his parents. They did not want to press charges.

The woman took her own life a few days later.

Many articles were written about her, and about why. Half the world forgave her, and half condemned. But everyone understood why.

Kidnapping became a common problem among the last children, as they came to be called. More and more, people (couples mostly) grew resentful and jealous of the parents of the last children. Until the last ones had to be isolated from the world at large. When David Pinkham was spotted? Everything would stop. People simply stared at him, enraptured. Whenever his security was breached, hordes of paparazzi would converge.

Entire magazines were devoted to his every childhood utterance and action. The world watched him grow up. All the last children were treated this way. But David, by far, was the most affected.

More years went by and no more children were born. Some took it as a sign from God, and made peace with themselves, and their neighbors, and awaited the end. Others raged. There was screaming and demanding Why? Never getting an answer, they took their hatred and frustration out on others. Ending their lives in a frenzy of denial, taking many with them.

A few trusted in science and human resourcefulness and patiently waited for them to make things right. Scientists and the technological elite quietly gathered the knowledge and wisdom of all mankind together. They looked for any clue as to what had happened.

As time went on, the last children came of age. David Pinkham married Susan Alvarez. She was born four days earlier than he was. The worldwide celebrations of their wedding lasted for days. A false era of hope dawned on humanity, despite the warnings of the scientists. It crumbled a year or two later. They were infertile as well.

Not even David Pinkham, whose name was known in every house and village, in every empty maternity ward, and every abandoned school–not even he could create a child.

That was the turning point. The moment the world truly understood. That it was over.

The people of earth at first despaired, then denied, and raged. And then despaired again. Whole religions sprang up where people knew in their hearts and souls, if they were good and pure enough, they would be given a child. Or maybe an explanation.

Some went the opposite extreme, reasoning that nothing mattered, so take what you want, there's no reason to leave anything behind.

Empires crumbled. Concepts like destiny, legacy, and history no longer had any meaning. Who cared what you accomplished, when no one would be around to remember?

In some places, monuments were erected, in hopes that other races, perhaps evolved apes or alien visitors, would know and remember Humanity. The wisdom and lore of the whole of mankind was sealed away in time vaults, hopefully designed to last millennia.

When David was forty, people had mostly grown accustomed to their fate. Genetics was the only science people were interested in. A few desperate people still tried to discover why and how.

The vast empires were gone. There was little interest in politics. What was the point? Suicides were commonplace, spoken of in passing resignation. Few holidays were noticed, let alone celebrated.

People stayed in touch for a long time, but slowly communications decayed. The satellites stopped working, the phone lines went down, even the Ham radios began to fail as parts became impossible to replace.

Animals were becoming common again. Dogs had begun to go feral more and more, as had cats. The wild things reclaimed the cities. People rarely lived there. The vast empty canyons of abandoned buildings were too big for the population, And their steel swingsets and wheel-a-rounds too much of a reminder.

The ones that were left preferred to gather in smaller places. A storm would break a dam, an earthquake ruin a once cherished landmark and no one would repair the damage. The forests and jungles were returning.

David Pinkham died at sixty eight. There weren't enough people interested in running a newspaper for it to be common knowledge. Nobody did an autopsy or examination to find out what he died of. Friends buried him, a few old men and women who wondered who would be the ones to bury them when their time came.

Nobody knew who was the last person to die, nobody was there to remember. No one knew what country he or she came from, what was the cause, how old he or she was. It didn't matter.

The judges of mankind began to arrive when there were no humans left. This time would be different. Mammals weren't the ones. Neither had been the reptiles. This was not the first time the judgment had been made on earth. The decision against reptiles had taken much longer than the ruling against mammals. Now they would try insects. The decision was reached quickly, only one hundred years of debate.

Cylinders were released, and the process begun again. Seventy two hours later, the tiny nano-constructs did their job.

All over the world, in anthills, beehives, and termite mounds, the droning sounds changed. The beings grew aware. Became thoughtful.

A new day was dawning.

Maybe this time, the judges conferred. This time. This time they'd do things the right way.

Third time's the charm.

www.ingramcontent.com/pod-product-compliance
Lightning Source LLC
Chambersburg PA
CBHW071254130626
46556CB00003B/1302